D1559952

BARNETT FRUMMER

IS AN UNBLOOMED FLOWER

ALSO BY CALVIN TRILLIN

An Education in Georgia

BARNETT FRUMMER IS AN UNBLOOMED FLOWER

NEW YORK / THE VIKING PRESS

And Other Adventures

of Barnett Frummer,

Rosalie Mondle, Roland Magruder,

and Their Friends

BY CALVIN TRILLIN

First published in 1969 by The Viking Press, Inc.
625 Madison Avenue, New York, N.Y. 10022

Published simultaneously in Canada by
The Macmillan Company of Canada Limited

Library of Congress catalog card number: 72–91199

Printed in U.S.A. by The Colonial Press

The following stories originally appeared in *The New Yorker*: "Barnett Frummer Is an Unbloomed Flower," "Barnett Frummer Learns to Distinguish Packaged Paprika from the Real Article," "Roland Magruder, Freelance Writer," "Barnett Frummer Accepts with Pleasure," "Barnett Frummer and Rosalie Mondle Meet Superman: A Love Story," and "Barnett Frummer Hears a Familiar Ring."

These stories were written for Alice

CONTENTS

BARNETT FRUMMER

IS AN UNBLOOMED FLOWER

Barnett Frummer
Is an Unbloomed Flower

The efforts of Barnett Frummer to become a successful radical were so consistently fruitless that his mentor, Roland Magruder, finally said, "Barnett, I'm afraid you might be one of the thousand flowers that's not going to bloom." (Roland, who had accused Mao Tse-tung of selling out to nonrevolutionary bureaucracy, nevertheless retained his old respect for Mao as a rhetorician.) Barnett felt like a flower not only unbloomed but also under attack by severe blight. He had spent months trying to impress Rosalie Mondle, whom he worshiped, with his radicalism, and Rosalie still treated him so much like part of the scenery that he sometimes imagined that someday, in an absent-minded moment, she might paint "Get Out of Vietnam" across his chest and shoulders.

His sacrifices on her behalf had been awesome. One blistering August day in Moline, Illinois, in a protest demonstration against discrimination in the Moline Housing Authority and Portuguese colonialism in Angola, he had gone limp for so long on the main street that his blue jeans adhered to the sticky asphalt; two hours after the other demonstrators had left to chain themselves to the door of the Moline City Hall, he was finally washed free by the spray of a street-cleaning machine. His weak arches had been so tortured by hundreds of miles of protest marching that he had been forced to wear his old Army boots everywhere, until Roland reminded him that they were a symbol of the military-industrial complex; at that point, he had taken to wearing high-top orthopedic shoes, which embarrassed him when he crossed his legs. And still the closest he ever seemed to get to Rosalie Mondle was in that brief moment when they passed each other while walking back and forth in a picket line—"like two ships in the night," Barnett lamented one afternoon to Roland Magruder.

"That reminds me," said Roland. "They need an extra pair of feet tonight to picket the Liberian ships loading grain for the Royalists in Yemen. Think your arches are up to it?"

"I just don't know anything anymore," said Barnett, eying the hated orthopedics. "I can't seem to *act*. Like I was going to refuse to pay my taxes as long as the tax money was used for weapons. Yesterday it turned out *they* owe *me* thirty-one dollars and twenty-five cents, and I don't know what to do about it. If I accept the refund, I'm dealing with them. If I refuse it, they'll use it for weapons, or at least some ammunition."

"Maybe you're not really alienated," Roland said.

"I don't think that's fair, Roland," said Barnett. "I'm as alienated as the next guy. It's just that I try to concentrate on the total bankruptcy of American liberal corporatism, and all I can see is Rosalie. I'm all for participatory democracy, but I need someone to participate *with*."

"Why don't you take my place as leader of the Liberian freighter demonstration?" Roland said. "If your feet get tired from picketing, you can talk everybody into throwing themselves across the path of the boat, and then you can float."

Barnett tried to refuse the offer, but Roland insisted, explaining that he himself was spending the entire evening picketing two Nationalist Chinese newspapers on Mott Street. Although he was still known in some circles as the brains behind the famous acerbic pamphlet "They're Selling Hot Buttered Popcorn in the China Lobby," Roland had long ago lost interest in Nationalist China. So far, however, he had been unable to find any Communist Chinese newspapers to picket.

It was a cool, misty evening on the Hoboken docks. Rosalie was the last person Barnett expected to see there, carrying a placard for the Committee to Protest American Commercial Involvement in Arab Wars (known also as the December 5th Movement, since the committee had been ejected without due process from its offices on December 5th for nonpayment of rent and telephone bill). It was not that Rosalie disagreed with the committee's aims. She agreed it should oppose the Royalists and support the efforts of a small deviationist faction of the Rebels led by Mohammed (Hands Off) Ahmed, a fiery leader who had earned his nickname by an alleged proclivity for cutting the hands off recalcitrant prisoners. However, not long after December 5th, the committee president had put his views in a telegram of protest to Washington, and Rosalie had immediately resigned, charging, in a celebrated letter, that "To send a telegram is to use the Establishment's own tools of communication and therefore to register an empty protest; you might as well campaign for the Democrats." But there she was, dressed in blue jeans and a paint-splattered sweat shirt, wearing a simple circle pin made of protest buttons, and carrying a sign that said "Hands Off Hands Off!"

Barnett was struck dumb by her grace and beauty. For several minutes, he could do no more than wave his placard weakly as he and Rosalie and half a dozen other pickets formed a moving oval on the dock. He was seriously considering the possibilities of approaching Rosalie directly and murmuring his "ships in the night" line—could he get in all those words in one pass?—when it occurred to him that militant leadership, not romanticism, was the most likely route to her heart. Summoning all of his courage, he suddenly shouted, "What about lying down in the path of the ship?"

6

It worked. Rosalie nodded vigorously, and said, "The Power Structure has to be confronted where you find it."

Barnett suddenly began to worry about the consequences of a float-in. The ship was not scheduled to leave port for two days, so lying down in its path represented a long-term commitment. He could not swim. But the picture of Rosalie following him into the oily water pushed these thoughts to the back of his mind. Her leader!

There was an enthusiastic buzz among the demonstrators as Rosalie crossed over to talk to Barnett. "In front of the ship is where it's at, all right," she said. "An act too radical for co-optation by the sellout Establishment liberals."

"It was nothing, really," said Barnett, beginning to wonder if the use of an inner tube would come under the heading of compromise. A few of the demonstrators had already discarded their shoes in preparation for the float-in. Barnett was now more worried about unlacing his orthopedic high-tops in front of the group than he was about not being able to stay afloat. But he was resolved to lead the pickets into the water. He would win the heart of Rosalie Mondle even if he drowned doing it.

At that moment, another group of demonstrators suddenly appeared on the dock—twenty neatly dressed young men and women marching in an orderly column of twos. One of them walked up to Barnett and said, "You must be Barnett Frummer, of the December 5th. I'm Howard Melton, of the East Sixties Reform Democratic Club. This is Cush Townsend, of the Mid-Sixties Modern Republicans.

We've decided to work as a team to protest this grain business."

"Hi, guy," said Cush Townsend, stepping out of the line to grab Barnett's hand.

"I think it's important and democratic to have coop-eration among militant protest groups," said Melton. "What we're hoping to do is to have both political parties adopt a pro-Hands Off policy in their Presidential plat-forms. We thought for a start we might lie down in front of the ship."

"Right, guy," said Townsend. He had already stripped down to a pair of madras swimming trunks. "Some of the guys brought masks. They thought they might get in a little scuba at the same time."

Barnett could not speak. Rosalie, however, was at no loss for words. "I'm surprised you forgot to call in the League of Women Voters," she said to Barnett. "I hear they're a regular bunch of bomb-throwers over there." Dropping her "Hands Off Hands Off!" placard at Bar-nett's feet, she stomped off the dock.

"How are things with you and Rosalie?" Roland asked the following afternoon.

"I didn't seem to handle the demonstration very well," said Barnett, unwilling to burden Roland with the dis-appointing details after all the trouble he had gone to.

"Have you heard from her?"

"At noon, a messenger brought me an application for the Ford Motor Company executive training program,"

Barnett replied sadly. "I think it was from her." Actually, the application, which might have been meant as the final cut, cheered Barnett a bit, since he had not previously been certain that Rosalie knew his name.

"Barnett," Roland said, "I think your trouble is that you don't have enough group militancy."

"There's only one of me," Barnett said.

"There is no room for smart alecks in the movement," said Roland. "Being cool is no longer cool, Barnett. Not being cool is cool."

"I'm sorry, I was upset," said Barnett. "How do you think I can get some group militancy?"

"Lead them right to the White House and go limp, naturally," said Roland. "Go to the Power Structure's main gate and lie down like a man. Let dozens of flowers bloom with you. Believe me, Rosalie will never be able to resist it."

Barnett had doubts about lying down at the White House, but he found it hard to resist anything that might give him a chance to impress Rosalie. Also, Roland had thought of a perfect occasion for going limp. The President had invited twenty bankers, four architects, and the film critic of the Orange County *Bulletin* to a Celebration of the North Atlantic Cultural Renaissance. What better time to demonstrate to the world the true radical's opposition to the American Establishment?

Barnett approached the administrative problems of the demonstration with a new-found ability to act. He scurried around to make arrangements with the chartered-bus company and the placard-maker; he notified the press and the Nazi Party. In a few weeks, the demonstration was ready. Fortunately, it was a bright, if somewhat chilly, day, and —even more welcome—Roland had apparently prevailed upon Rosalie to join the demonstration. She was, in fact, the first one down as the group spread itself across the White House driveway to block the Cadillacs carrying those invited to the celebration. Barnett was ecstatic.

The cars had been held up for about twenty minutes when two White House guards approached Barnett, ascertained that he was the leader of the demonstration, and told him that the President would like to see him. The demonstrators were jubilant as Barnett walked away with the guards. "Tell him, Barnett!" they shouted. "Give it to him, Barney baby!" Barnett waved and pulled his blue jeans lower, to cover his orthopedic shoes. Pressed against the gate, the demonstrators saw a man come out of the White House to meet Barnett. He shook Barnett's hand and walked him back to the White House. The demonstrators strained to hear the conversation, but all they heard was "I think all Americans want to make the same thing perfectly clear, Mr. Frummer," and then the two figures disappeared into the White House.

Thirty minutes later, Barnett emerged and walked to the gate to address his followers. "I think we've reached a good agreement," he said, speaking with unaccustomed confidence. "I have told the President that I will remove the demonstrators from the gate, and in return he has agreed to schedule a Festival of Radicalism in America at the White House sometime next fall. He suggested we join him in a Crusade Against the Establishment."

"Sellout!" somebody yelled.

"Fink!" yelled another demonstrator.

Barnett was stunned. "I don't think you realize what kind of help a man that important can give us in fighting the Power Structure!" he shouted.

But the demonstrators were outraged. They would have refused to leave, except that Barnett had already ordered the buses, and there was no other way to get back to New York free. Some ladies from the White House served hot chocolate and club sandwiches to the demonstrators as they lined up to file onto the buses.

Rosalie Mondle seemed the angriest of all. She refused to board the bus, and she would have had to spend the long day in Washington alone, except that Roland Magruder happened to be in the area interviewing some Albanian revisionists. He and Rosalie went limp together in a small anteroom of the South African Embassy, where it was cozy and warm.

Barnett Frummer Learns to Distinguish Packaged Paprika from the Real Article

Whenever there was a remote chance that Barnett Frummer might find himself in the presence of Rosalie Mondle —whom he worshiped, almost entirely from afar—he frantically prepared for a witty conversation about politics and the arts, although he was aware that her proximity usually made him speechless.

"What's the latest thing?" he often asked his friend and mentor Roland Magruder. "Just in case it comes up." When, through some complicated machinations, he managed to be included in a dinner party to which Marshall and Madeline Slovin had invited Elliot and Myrna Nardling, Lester Drentluss, and Rosalie Mondle, he was, thanks to Roland, fully prepared.

"I suppose, in a way, China is really doing what she's been doing for centuries, nothing more, nothing less," Barnett began tentatively, as they were having drinks.

"What marvelous cocktail knishes!" Myrna Nardling said, after popping one into her mouth.

"I think the idea that the only relevant theater is political theater is not entirely without merit," Barnett said.

"Marshall drove all the way to Yonah Schimmel's Knishery to get them," Madeline said proudly.

"Uptown or downtown branch?" Elliot Nardling asked.

Madeline stopped to think, permitting Barnett time to make a quick remark about the economic implications of air pollution. "It must have been downtown," she finally said. "It was way down on Houston Street."

"Uptown," Rosalie said, smiling. "I thought so. The downtown is on Delancey, but it closed last year. I always thought that the knishes were a touch lighter at the downtown, but, of course, there are two schools of thought on that one."

"The question of ethnic groups maintaining cultural identities in New York is really two-edged," Barnett said.

"Somebody has taken some trouble with this *homus*, Madeline," Lester Drentluss said, spreading another thick layer on his freshly baked sesame cracker. "Mash your own chick-peas, I suppose."

Barnett was puzzled. The Lester Drentluss he knew had always considered any drinking occasion enhanced by the presence of onion-flavored dip.

"Well, actually, it's from the wife of a little Syrian

grocer in Borough Park," Madeline said, looking as if the only vegetable she wanted to mash was Lester Drentluss.

"It's nice to get around the city," Barnett said, but he felt he had somehow missed the line of conversation.

He became convinced of it after they had gone in for dinner. Marshall and Madeline talked so much about the preparation of the meal that they hardly had time to eat. Rosalie looked fascinated while Madeline told of the chicken farm near Center Moriches and the apple orchard near Poughkeepsie that had made possible her main course of Chicken Vallée d'Auge with Sautéed Apple Rings. Barnett almost nodded off to sleep while Marshall spoke for twenty minutes about how his hand-turned coffee grinder avoided the "electric taste" of an automatic coffee grinder —an explanation that coincided precisely with the time it took him to grind the coffee. After coffee, they pushed back their chairs, and Madeline, gracefully accepting the compliments of her guests, said, "There's just no substitute for peeling asparagus, no matter what they say."

"Neatness counts," Barnett said, smiling at Rosalie.

Rosalie responded with one of the exasperated sighs that Barnett always heard in his nightmares about her just before he woke up.

"Anything edible they don't grind themselves they have a little man for," Roland Magruder explained to Barnett the next afternoon, as they shared a quart bottle of Schlitz and some barbecue-flavored potato chips. "You're going to have to find a few little men and memorize a few beef-stroganoff recipes. Let the State Department worry about China for a while. And don't let Madeline Slovin scare you. I hear she uses canned leeks."

Barnett had never been seriously interested in food. At one point in his life, he had lived mostly on frozen pizza, frozen macaroni-and-cheese, and a favorite of his called La Bomba Frozen Mexican Combination TeeVee Taco Dinner. Most evenings, he would transfer a La Bomba Dinner from the ice-cube compartment of the refrigerator to the oven and, during the thawing process, dream of the day when he and Rosalie would sit at their own kitchen table, arguing affectionately about who would have the taco and who the enchilada. He never ate any vegetables— a situation that began to worry him when, feeling a bit out of sorts, he went to the doctor and was told that he had a Vitamin-B$_1$ deficiency that could eventually make him the only young executive in midtown Manhattan with pellagra. Concerned about his health, Barnett briefly considered trying to prepare what he always thought of as his "first thawed dish," but then he discovered frozen vegetables. He used the kind wrapped in plastic bags that are dropped into boiling water, and he kept a large pot of water on the stove permanently, like a French housewife cooking a *pot-au-feu*. Occasionally, he would bring the water to a boil and drop in a bag of turnips or Green Giant Mexicorn. Barnett changed the water every week—on Wednesdays, when he put fresh water in the fishbowl. He had no idea how anybody would peel asparagus without tearing open the plastic bag.

After his conference with Roland, though, Barnett bought fifty dollars' worth of cookbooks, traced a special list of import licenses that Roland had suspected would exist in the City Markets Commissioner's office, and began to learn about food and little men. He found a little man on Elizabeth Street who imported hybrid shallots, and a little man on Atlantic Avenue who sold Mykonosian halvah, and a little man in Yonkers who baked fresh cornflakes. Sometimes, as he took notes on Julia Child's lettuce-washing instructions on television or shuddered at Roy Andries de Groot's description of the kind of people who permit ready-ground nutmeg in their kitchens, his thoughts would wander toward Rosalie Mondle. He could picture her spending a quiet evening at home weaving special filters for her Chemex coffee-maker, or standing in her kitchen growing her own chervil and splitting her own peas. He wondered if she ground her own cleanser.

Only six months after he began studying, Barnett had his first opportunity to test his knowledge. Elliot and Myrna Nardling were having a small dinner party, and both Rosalie and Barnett were invited. "Don't worry about Myrna," Roland told him that afternoon. They were having a strategy session over some Kraft American–cheese sandwiches at Roland's. "They tell me her *arugula* is often a bit dampish."

"Good bread, Myrna," Barnett said that evening, as he included a bite of it with a forkful of the Braised Haunch of Wild Boar Prince de Chimay she had prepared.

"Thanks," Myrna said coldly.

"I happened to find a new place for bread myself," Barnett went on. "I smelled some baking as I was walking down Hester Street on the way to my celery store. A little man named Galabrino bakes it in the back of his vinegar shop. No sign, of course, and barely speaks English."

"Is that A. Galabrino?" Elliot Nardling asked.

"Could be. Why?"

"I think he's been written up in *Vogue* a couple of times in the 'People Are Talking About' column."

"Must be another Galabrino," Barnett said.

"I don't think so," Rosalie said. "Randy Michaelman knew his son at Andover."

Barnett thought he was about to hear her sigh. "Well, it wasn't as good as this, anyway," he said.

When Barnett got home that night, he pulled Volume II of his *Gourmet Cookbook* from the shelf—he was working his way through it slowly, memorizing recipes—but the instructions for Paupiettes de Bœuf Braisées Bourbonnaise seemed hopelessly complicated, and he went to sleep long before he had completed his ninety-minute quota. He did not sleep well. The Braised Haunch of Wild Boar Prince de Chimay seemed to have disagreed with him, and he thought all the talk about wine that evening might have made him slightly drunk, although he couldn't remember how many glasses he had had. He felt as if he had a fever. As he stared at the ceiling, he began to imagine himself leading Rosalie Mondle to a little man who sold Polish *kielbasa* sausages, only to find out that she stuffed her own. Then he imagined himself bringing her a recipe for mixing her own Indonesian *nasi goreng* curry, only to discover that she had a little man for it. Little men seemed to walk back and forth in front of his eyes, cursing him in broken English and grinding things all over the floor. He saw himself at an awesomely expensive store sending out a package containing a Milanese *pasta* machine, a Moroccan *couscoussière,* and a card that said, "I cannot live without you. Barnett." He was buying Rosalie a copper mold in the shape of a wildebeest. He kept asking her if she liked the gifts, but all she said was "What is more delicious/ Than knishes?" Roland was there suddenly. "Did you get a good look at her artichoke hearts?" he was saying. "I hear they have the taste of the jar about them." The Nardlings and the Slovins were dancing around Barnett in a great circle, pelting him with stuffed mushrooms. "Barnett uses ketchup!" they chanted. "Barnett uses ketchup!" Somebody kept feeding him. "Eat this Paupiettes de Bœuf Braisées Bourbonnaise or go to bed without your supper," the feeder said. "Have another knish. Have *another* knish." Lester Drentluss was standing at a pegboard, giving a lecture on Barnett. "Barnett Frummer often eats Fritos," Lester was saying, pointing to a bag of Fritos with a wire whisk. Barnett groaned and covered his face with his pillow, but he could hear the Nardlings and the Slovins taking up the chant about Fritos. Rosalie smiled and nodded in agreement, although she kept repeating, "What is more delicious/Than knishes?" Barnett was being chased by a wild boar ridden by an arrogant-looking man who was wearing a slim double-breasted pin-striped suit. "Isn't that the Prince de Chimay?" Rosalie said, touching her hair to make sure it was in place.

Toward dawn, he thought he was falling asleep, and it seemed only a few minutes later when the phone rang. It was Roland. "Don't worry about last night," Roland said. "I think I just discovered a sure way of telling Julia Child's *coq au vin* from Michael Field's *coq au vin*. You'll sweep her off her feet when she hears that one."

"I think I'd just as soon not talk about it now," Barnett said, wondering if he would feel any better if he stood up. "I really think Rosalie would be more impressed by some insights into China, if I could just figure out a better way of getting into the history."

After he hung up, he went into the kitchen. He stopped to fill up the water pot, and tried to remember if he still had any Green Giant Mexicorn in the freezer.

Roland Magruder,
Free-Lance Writer

During the first week of summer, at a beach party in East Hampton, a portly man wearing tan Levi's and a blue-and-white gondolier's shirt told Marlene Nopkiss that he was a "socioeconomic observer" currently working on a study entitled "The Appeal of Chinese Food to Jewish Intellectuals." Marlene had already suggested that the rejection of one dietary ritual might lead inevitably to the adoption of another when it occurred to her that he might not be telling the truth. Later in the evening, she was informed that the man was in fact the assistant accountant of a trade magazine catering to the pulp-and-paper industry. She was more cautious a few days later, nodding without commitment when a man she met at a grocery store in Amagansett said he spent almost all of his time "banging away at the old novel." A few days later, she saw his picture in an advertisement that a life-insurance company had taken in the New York *Times* to honor its leading salesmen in the New York-New Jersey-Connecticut area. She eventually decided that men automatically misrepresent their occupations in the summer on the eastern end of Long Island, as if some compulsion to lie were hanging in the air just east of Riverhead. The previous summer, in another Long Island town, everybody had said he was an artist of one kind or another; the year before that, in a town not ten miles away, men had claimed to be mystical wizards of the New York Stock Exchange. Around East Hampton, she seemed to meet nobody who did not claim to be a writer. When Marlene drove past the Sunday-morning softball game in East Hampton, she was fond of saying—even though she was invariably alone—"There stand eighteen free-lance writers, unless they're using short-fielders today, in which case there stand twenty free-lance writers." Marlene was beginning to pride herself on her cynicism.

Occasionally, she met writers who were not free-lance writers, since they were employed by some magazine or newspaper, but they all said that their jobs meant nothing more to them than a way to finance their real writing—and they demonstrated this fact with stories about their office heresies. One of them—a slim young man who said his real writing was "a children's book for adults about a boy and girl in Carl Schurz Park"—told Marlene that he wrote the Religion section for *Time* and that he drove the editors to distraction by putting the word "alleged" before all questionable religious events, so that he would write, "The Gospels were written fifty years after the alleged Crucifixion," or "The Jews wandered in the wilderness for forty years after the alleged parting of the Red Sea." Marlene realized that the alleged writer did not in fact write the Religion section of *Time* when she finally placed his face as belonging to one of the countless Wall Street wizards she had met two summers before. It turned out he was neither a Wall Street wizard nor a Religion writer but a salesman who tried to sign up young executives for the Alexander Hamilton Business Course. Marlene was not surprised. A week later, she dismissed with one loud guffaw a young man who said he conquered the anonymity of the *Newsweek* National Affairs section by spelling out "LOOK, MA, IT'S ME, IRV" vertically with the first letter of the first word in each paragraph of his stories.

Not long after she had disposed of the would-be Religion writer, she met a man named Arnold Kranitt, who said he supported himself while writing his novel by working for a company called After Dinner, Inc. According to Kranitt, After Dinner, Inc. earned a great deal of money by providing after-dinner speakers with well-written speeches on any subject. "It's really *too* sordid," said Kranitt, smiling at the recollection. "I work for a very crude man who never says anything to me but 'Hey, champ, can you knock me out eight hundred words on the place of foundation garments in our private enterprise system by six tonight?' or 'Hey, champ, why don't you sit

yourself down and work me up the two thousand words
Eddie O'Brien will have to say at a testimonial dinner
called Eddie O'Brien's Twenty-five Years Behind the
Wheel of a Five-Passenger Checker, by ten tomorrow
morning?' "

Marlene listened to Kranitt for about ten minutes before
recognizing him as a man who had once waited on her at
Bloomingdale's. She said, "Listen, champ, why don't you
knock me out fifty words on brushing off a phony." If he
had been a decent phony, she thought later, he would
have at least quoted her a price for a brush-off speech.

After all these experiences, Marlene was understandably
skeptical when, at a party at Bernie and Greta Mohler's
summer place near East Hampton, a young man named
Roland Magruder answered her question about his occupation in the usual way. "What *kind* of writer?" she said,
suspiciously. She could not believe that he had not heard
how difficult she was to impress with this approach.

"A free-lance writer," said Magruder, who was quite
aware of how difficult she was to impress with this approach, and had even heard odds quoted on the matter.

"What kind of free-lance writer?" asked Marlene.

"A sign writer."

"A sign painter?"

"No," said Magruder. "I write signs. Cities retain me to
write signs on a free-lance basis. I specialize in traffic work.
'Yield Right of Way' is a good example."

"Somebody *wrote* 'Yield Right of Way'?" asked Marlene.

"*I* wrote 'Yield Right of Way,' " said Magruder, permitting a tone of pride to creep into his voice. "Do you think something like 'Yield Right of Way' writes itself? Do you think it was written by the gorilla who installed the signs on the Expressway? He would have probably written 'Let the Other Guy Keep in Front of Ya.' Have you been going under the impression that 'Vehicles Weighing Over Five Tons Keep Right' was composed by John V. Lindsay?"

"But these messages are obvious," argued Marlene.

"You would have probably said that it was obvious for Brigham Young to say 'This is the place' when the Mormons reached Utah, or for Pétain to say 'They shall not pass,' or for MacArthur to say 'I shall return.' I suppose you think those lines just happened to come out of their mouths, without any previous thought or professional consultation. I think, by the way, if I may say so, that my 'No Passing' says everything 'They shall not pass' says, and without succumbing to prolixity."

"You mean to say you're being paid for writing 'Stop' and 'One Way' and 'Slow'?" asked Marlene. She tried to include as much sarcasm as possible in her voice, but Magruder seemed to take no notice.

"A certain economy of style has never been a handicap to a writer," he said. "On the other hand, while it's true that traffic signs are a vehicle that permits a pithiness impossible in most forms, I do longer pieces. 'Next Train for Grand Central on Track Four' is one of mine—at the Times Square subway station. There's another one at the Times Square station that you certainly haven't seen yourself but that I think has a certain flair: 'This Is Your Men's Room; Keep It Clean.' I've heard several people talk of that one as the ultimate expression of man's inability to identify with his group in an urban society."

That was almost too much for Marlene. She had found herself beginning to believe Magruder—his self-confidence was awesome, and, after all, who would have the gall to take credit for "One Way" if he hadn't written it?—but bringing in sociological criticism was a challenge to credulity. Just then, Bernie Mohler passed by on his way to the patio and said, "Nice job on 'Shea Stadium Parking,' Roland."

"What did you have to do with Shea Stadium Parking?" asked Marlene.

"That's it," said Magruder. " 'Shea Stadium Parking.' It's on the Expressway. Do you like it?"

Before Marlene could answer, a blond girl joined them and asked, "Was that your 'This Is Water Mill—Slow Down and Enjoy It' I saw on Highway 27, Roland?"

Magruder frowned. "I'm not going to get involved in that cutesy stuff just to satisfy the Chamber of Commerce types," he said. "I told the town board that 'Slow Down' says it all, and they could take it or leave it."

"I thought your 'No Parking Any Time' said it all," remarked a tall young man with a neat beard. "I've heard a lot of people say so."

"Thanks very much," Magruder said, looking down at the floor modestly.

"Oh, did you do that?" Marlene found herself asking.

"It wasn't much," said Magruder, still looking at the floor.

"You don't happen to know who did the big 'NO' sign at Coney Island?" Marlene asked. "The one that has one 'NO' in huge letters and then lists all the things you can't do in smaller letters next to it?" Marlene realized she had always been interested in the big 'NO' sign.

"I introduced the Big 'NO' concept at the city parks several years ago," said Magruder. "Some people say it's a remarkable insight into modern American urban life, but I think that kind of talk makes too big a thing of it."

"Oh, I don't," said Marlene. "I think it's a marvelous expression of the negativism of our situation."

"Well, that's enough talking about me," said Magruder. "Can I get you another drink?"

"I'm really tired of this party anyway," said Marlene.

"I'll drive you home," said Magruder. "We can cruise by a 'Keep Right Except to Pass' sign, if you like. It's on the highway just in front of my beach house."

"Well, O.K.," said Marlene, "but no stopping."

"I wrote that," Magruder said, and they walked out the door together.

Barnett Frummer
Accepts with Pleasure

When Barnett Frummer examined his failure to capture the heart of Rosalie Mondle—an examination he carried on approximately six hours each day—it often occurred to him that the only place he could count on seeing Rosalie was at one of Elliot Nardling's parties. In his more realistic moments, Barnett realized that he could not even count on that, because he was not always invited to Elliot Nardling's parties. Elliot had what was widely considered an admirable loyalty to Barnett, an old college friend, but Elliot's wife, Myrna Nardling, was one of the best-known hostesses in Manhattan, and it was often said that she never had more than two people at a party to whom any reasonably well-informed person would dare address the question "What do you do?" Elliot's obligation to his relatives, who were undistinguished but rich, meant that both slots were often occupied. No one would need to ask Rosalie what she did. She always seemed to be in the columns—taking part in a boutique opening or a civil-rights demonstration, or being escorted someplace by some performer who was a smash hit somewhere (*smashed* hit, Barnett always muttered to himself when he saw one of those)—and she was a steady visitor at the Nardlings'. Often when Barnett read in the columns about who was enjoying Rosalie's company at a dinner party Elliot and Myrna Nardling had given the night before—a night he had likely spent calculating how he might nonchalantly alight from a Fifth Avenue bus in front of Rosalie's apartment house at exactly the time she was emerging to walk her dog—he began to feel as if he would never be invited anywhere, not even to every fifteenth or twentieth party at the Nardlings'. He realized, as he looked over the columns one day, that he would never be in a position not to be asked what he did, and he was certainly not in a good position when he *was* asked what he did. Who was interested in a family awning business? The night before, Rosalie had been mixing with, among others, René Plenet, the fashion photographer and blank-verse poet; the Contessa di Puglia; four out of five members of the Cretins, the most popular British singing group appearing in the city; and Rolly Rawlings, the most vibrant political force in the Nardlings' set, a lady whose picture had been taken by the *Times* the previous day as she supported the California grape boycott by standing in front of an East Side supermarket handing out the

Huelga! buttons she always carried around in a Gucci shopping bag. What could he ever do to compete with people like that?

"Never compete," Barnett was told one afternoon by Roland Magruder. "The only way to beat these party people is to refuse to go to parties." Roland had chosen that device himself, and it always seemed to Barnett that his friend accomplished as much by refusing to attend a party as most people did by spending an entire evening at one. "They wanted me to come to one of those phony, boring all-night pot smokers at Bergwort's," he would say, mentioning the most sought-after novelist-playwright in the city. "I told them there was a surfing movie I wanted to see that evening before it left the nabes for good." Roland had refused invitations to some of the most important homes in the city, and he often spent his afternoon going through the columns and sneering at the people he had refused to mingle with the night before. He was occasionally mentioned in the columns as someone who was not present at some otherwise celebrity-laden event.

Refusing to go to parties was hardly the answer for Barnett Frummer. In the first place, he pointed out to Roland, a person had to be invited before he could refuse. And if this happened by any chance—that is, if any of his old college friends besides Elliot Nardling became a host—he could hardly give up a possible opportunity to see Rosalie just to make a gesture. The other obvious solution—becoming a host himself—was also out of the question. Even if he possessed the other qualifications, he would be disqualified by the fact that financially the awning trade had been only moderately good to him. Elliot Nardling was fortunate enough to have a father who was a well-known hair-net manufacturer with deep show-business connections, and the old man was perfectly happy to have his son devote full time to what Elliot called "the profession of catalyzing the celebrated" as long as he promised to stay away from the profession of manufacturing hair nets.

"Which is why I suggest that you become an adviser," Roland told Barnett.

"You mean read tea leaves and that sort of thing?" asked Barnett. "There already is one in the Nardlings' set."

"Of course that's not what I mean," said Roland. "How do you think these hostesses know which people to ask? Do you realize the administrative problems of keeping up with who the hot people are—just in newspaper reading alone? It's a job for a specialist. As it happens, I know a girl —Wendy Olswang by name—who is very interested in becoming a hostess. She has a duplex apartment, a few connections, an independent alimony, and a thick skin. I've taken the liberty of suggesting you as an adviser."

Barnett gratefully accepted Roland's offer. He had a vacation coming up, and then it would be winter, always a slow season in the awning business. In that time, he might be able to lure Rosalie to one or two parties, or even—how could such developments be predicted?—organize an entire season of parties that Rosalie would find positively magnetic. He had, of course, no knowledge of party-giving techniques, except the Nardlings' two-unknowns formula, but he was aware that the guiding principle of choosing people to invite to parties was similar to the one governing the purchase of fruit and vegetables: get them just when they're ripe. He met Wendy Olswang for lunch that Monday, and, applying the guiding principle directly, advised his client to give a dinner party the following Saturday night in honor of the young novelist whose book had received the front-page review in the *Times Book Review* the day before.

To Barnett's amazement, the process of organizing the party seemed relatively simple. With a daring he had not previously noticed in himself, he phoned the novelist and, by hinting strongly of Wendy's connections with producers interested in buying thin novels for big movies, persuaded him to be the guest of honor. Then, straining Wendy's contacts to the limit, he put together a nicely balanced guest list that included the most prominent film actor in the peace movement, one of the leading Mafia lawyers in New York, a Lower East Side minister with Upper East Side connections, a brace of English hairdressers, the heavyweight wrestling champion of the world, and Rosalie Mondle, girl-about-town. All of them refused.

"I can't understand it," said Barnett, lamenting to Roland Magruder the morning after he and Wendy Olswang had spent a long Saturday evening trying to explain to a sullen young novelist that they really preferred intimate dinner parties. "His book had the *frontpage review* in the *Times* book-review section on Sunday."

33

"When was that?" asked Roland casually.

"This last Sunday," said Barnett, puzzled at the question.

"Never invite from the Sunday *Times* book section after it's come out," said Roland. "Myrna Nardling sends Elliot to a special newsstand on Lexington Avenue on Wednesdays, because it gets the book section of the Sunday *Times* three days early. She had a party last night in honor of the philosopher whose book had the front-page review in the *Times* book section today. You were entertaining last week's author."

"I should have known," said Barnett. "He seemed all used up."

"Don't feel let down, Barnett," Roland said, in a kindly tone. "The Nardling party was obviously a bore. Myrna wanted me to come, and I told her I thought I'd stay home and watch Jackie Gleason on television. I get a kick out of him occasionally."

Barnett felt let down nonetheless. He had planned to spend the early evening strolling past a Broadway movie theater—there was a *première* scheduled, and, according to his calculations, Rosalie might show up from eight to eleven minutes early, depending on the traffic—but he was too depressed to leave his apartment. To his surprise, Wendy Olswang phoned to say that she was willing to continue her effort to become a hostess. Barnett didn't think he could face it, although visions of greeting Rosalie as the acknowledged organizer of a gay, witty dinner party still flashed through his head as Wendy talked. "It's been so long," he would say casually, kissing Rosalie on the cheek as he took her wrap. "The Contessa has talked about nothing but you all night. What can I get you to drink? Have you seen good old Elliot and Myrna lately? What *is* Elliot doing now?"

"What a marvelous party," she would say. "Aren't the Cretins just too much, pouring their drinks on the Contessa that way? Doesn't Rolly Rawlings look absolutely marvelous in her tin pants suit? René Plenet is such a blank-verse bore. It's been so long, Barnett. You've been off doing something exciting, I suppose. You're so—"

"How about a picnic?" Wendy was saying on the phone.

"I wouldn't advise that," said Barnett, emerging slowly from his fantasy.

"I'm so glad you're my adviser again," Wendy said.

"We advisers can't work miracles, but I'll see what I can do," said Barnett. What did he have to lose?

In the weeks that followed, Barnett worked night after night trying to advise a party that Rosalie Mondle would attend. By Christmas, through almost superhuman effort, he had managed to plan six parties for Wendy Olswang. They drew a total of eleven guests, three of whom had not been invited but spotted the coat rack in the hall from the elevator. During the same period, Myrna Nardling's house seemed to be constantly filled with celebrities as she gave parties for an avant-garde filmmaker who had just become famous with the release of *Nostril*, a four-and-a-half-hour film consisting of a totally black screen and the sound of breathing; a new ambassador whose appointment she had learned of through an agent she maintained in the State Department at some expense; and the author of the latest smash-hit Broadway comedy, *Naked, Naked!* (Myrna had stayed up late to read the reviews and had extended her invitation during a supposedly accidental meeting with the playwright near the door of his apartment house as he returned from the opening-night party at six the following morning.)

Barnett Frummer gazed at the picture of Rosalie Mondle he kept on his dresser—it was a newspaper photo of Rosalie leaving a night club with a United States senator, a fabulously successful sixteen-year-old designer of African earrings for men, and a pretender to the Serbian throne—and he thought about giving up. At that moment, the phone rang. It was a newspaper reporter. Barnett thought the man had the wrong Frummer, but the reporter assured him that he, Barnett Frummer, was getting so well-known around town for his "amusing and burlesque adventures as a party adviser" that he would make a perfect subject for an interview. The interview appeared the next morning, but even before that—late the same night, in fact, just a few minutes after the early editions were put on the trucks—Barnett received a call from Myrna Nardling. She thought it would be nice if he were the guest of honor at a little dinner she was giving Saturday night. Nothing formal, just the usual crowd.

"So nice to see you," Myrna said at the door, kissing Barnett on the cheek. "It's been so long. Scott Kulchek, the racing driver, has been talking of nothing else but that marvelous piece on you."

"What a marvelous party!" said Barnett. "Nice to see the Cretins again; they're a kick. I remember the time Rosalie Mondle said to them—Is she here, by the way?"

"No, she's not," said Myrna, with some irritation. "I asked her, of course."

"I suppose she's got an opening or something," Barnett said. His disappointment was somewhat blunted by the knowledge that, being on the circuit himself now, he would probably see her at the next party.

"No, as a matter of fact she said she's staying home to help Roland Magruder sew some insignia on his Army Reserve uniforms," said Myrna. "But come in the living room and hear the poem René Plenet has written about you."

"Marvelous party," mumbled Barnett. "It's been so long." He wondered how long he'd have to stay. Before Myrna phoned, he had been working out a mathematical equation on the percentages of ending up in the same elevator with Rosalie if he started going to a dentist in the building her office was in, and he was anxious to get back to his figures.

Barnett Frummer and Rosalie Mondle Meet Superman: A Love Story

In the late afternoon of a Sunday that had been painfully uneventful, Barnett Frummer happened upon the discovery that Ted Mack's "Original Amateur Hour" was Pop, and maybe even Camp. It came when he idly switched on the television set and saw two middle-aged ladies from Ohio, accompanied by a pianist, playing "Buckle Down, Winsocki" by pulling window shades up and down on portable window frames. He knew immediately that he might be looking at his breakthrough into tastemaking, which he had been dreaming about for two years, and he caught himself about to say "Eureka!" Instead, he said, "Holy Moly." (He had once read in the *Wyoming Quarterly* that the reason Billy Batson took the time to say "Holy Moly" just before somebody tightened a gag on his mouth to prevent him from saying "Shazam!" and thus turning into Captain Marvel was that his mouth was open in surprise, allowing him freedom of aspiration but not of sibilance. Barnett, who had attended seminars on Billy Batson, had spotted the error immediately and had written the *Quarterly* a long letter explaining that although Billy said "Holy Moly" at other times, usually when he was dumfounded at the mores of the society around him, he never said anything except "Sha—" just before somebody tightened a gag on his mouth to prevent him from saying "Shazam!" Barnett had counted on the letter being his breakthrough, but the correspondence column in the *Wyoming Quarterly* that month had been taken up entirely by a well-known poet's essay on Victor Mature, and his letter had never been printed.)

When Barnett's idea struck him, he immediately reached for the copies of *Partisan Review* and *Life* he kept by his bed for consultation. Formerly, Barnett had depended on *Partisan Review* alone for cultural guidance, but when its subject matter became the same as *Life*'s he took out a subscription to *Life* so he could see pictures of what *Partisan Review* was talking about. He turned to the *Life* article by Rosalind Constable on Pop styles and read, ". . . anything can get into the Pop act, provided it is contemporary, corny, or known from coast to coast." Without reaching for his *TV Guide*—a magazine he still kept around despite its rejection of his panegyric on Tab Hunter—Barnett knew that Ted Mack's "Original Amateur Hour" was on network television, and had been for years. It was easily Pop, he thought, studying the *Life* definition, but was it Camp? *Partisan Review* fell open at his touch to the article on Camp by Susan Sontag —an article that had long ago been covered with Barnett's neat underlinings. "When something is just bad (rather than Camp)," he read, "it's often because it is too mediocre in its ambition. The artist hasn't attempted to do anything really outlandish. ('It's too much,' 'It's fantastic,' 'It's not to be believed' are standard phrases of Camp enthusiasm.)"

The two ladies on television were still in the first chorus of "Buckle Down, Winsocki," but one of them had added a Venetian blind to her window shade, and she was opening and closing it rhythmically with one hand while continuing the up-and-down motion of the window shade with the other. "Gak!" Barnett thought, incidentally complimenting himself on remembering what Donald Duck always said in moments of stress. "What ambition! It's not to be believed!" He looked more closely at the two ladies, who were becoming breathless in their efforts to keep the window shades and Venetian blind moving in rhythm. Was he feeling the "sensibility of failed seriousness, of the theatricalization of experience" that Miss Sontag had written about? He thought he was. But was the performance really naïve enough to be "pure Camp"? He had always maintained that he did not need Susan Sontag to tell him that "the traditional means for going beyond straight seriousness—irony, satire—seem feeble today, inadequate to the culturally over-saturated medium in which contemporary sensibility is schooled." There was, however, nothing ironic about the two ladies on the "Original Amateur Hour." Their faces were grim, and they took great deep breaths as the tempo of the music increased and the window shades went up and down more rapidly. There was but one more test. The *Partisan Review* article had said that "homosexuals, by and large, constitute the vanguard—and the most articulate audience—of Camp." And, "the androgyne is certainly one of the great images of Camp sensibility." The two ladies were in the last chorus of "Buckle Down, Winsocki." Both of them were manipulating Venetian blinds as well as window shades now, and the slightly heavier one was standing on one foot, using the other foot to beat time against the window frame. They were going so fast that the pianist was having to skip notes to keep up. Barnett moved to within a few inches of the screen and studied the ladies. The more he stared at them, the more androgynous they became. "Holy Moly!" he said aloud. Then, despite his excitement, he remembered Wonder Woman, and changed that to "Great Hera!"

Barnett's previous efforts at becoming a tastemaker had resulted in unrelieved and humiliating failure. He had often considered giving it all up. Then he would look at the snapshot of Rosalie Mondle he kept on his desk—it was in the place of honor between the pictures of Gene Autry and Alice Faye he had picked up, with their frames, in an out-of-the-way dime store—and he would be seized with new determination. He had taken the picture of Rosalie secretly at a party. She had been talking about the works of Albert Payson Terhune with Lester Drentluss, and she had the confident look of someone who knew she was an acknowledged expert.

Barnett's efforts were all for Rosalie; she could respect only a tastemaker. Once, through a friend in the advertising business, Barnett had acquired a long-playing medley of advertisting jingles written by Richard Adler, including three versions of the Newport cigarette song (jazz, cha-cha, and romantic), but everybody in the group had scorned it as completely unnaïve. Then he started collecting authorized histories of companies and organizations. One night, when the whole gang went to the roller derby, he casually complained of being tired because he had stayed up all night reading "Young Men Can Change the World: The Story of the Junior Chamber of Commerce," a book he said he considered superior to "Of Lasting Interest: The Story of the Reader's Digest," and altogether just too much. But everybody seemed to think that "Young Men Can Change the World: The Story of the Junior Chamber of Commerce" was not too much at all. "Barely enough," Rosalie said. Barnett could not seem to shake the reputation of being a follower. In fact, the reputation was so strong that he began to suspect that he himself was being tolerated by his more sophisticated friends as a piece of Camp. The suspicion grew in his mind when he thought he overheard Rosalie say, "That Barnett is just fantastic. He's really not to be believed." That night, Barnett almost gave up. Sleepless, he spent most of the night trying to lose himself in the mechanics of pasting clippings in the scrapbook he kept on former Queens of the Pulaski Day Parade. But it was no use; he was tortured by thoughts of failure. Morning, however, brought a new look at the picture of Rosalie, and new courage.

Barnett had first been introduced to Camp when he left a West Side party with someone he had taken to be a very good-looking young lady but who later turned out to be his old college roommate, Roland Magruder. Roland had thrown off his disguise right away and taken Barnett to a nearby bar to lecture him on how to become a tastemaker. "I myself am so heterosexual it's fantastic," Roland had said, "but if the ticket of admission to the avant-garde is an occasional pair of high heels, I say pay it." Wanting very much to be part of the avant-garde himself, Barnett had eagerly accepted Roland's invitation to audit meetings of the Batman Club, an all-male organization that met in the back of a Scopitone bar every Wednesday to discuss what the *Wyoming Quarterly* had called "the nature of the relationship between partners in the various 'partners against crime' found in the comic books of the middle forties."

Now, two years later, despite all Roland Magruder's impeccable advice, Barnett Frummer was still considered a follower. And despite all Roland Magruder's learned counseling on how to capture the heart of Rosalie Mondle, Barnett Frummer seemed to mean nothing to her—or, if he had overheard her correctly, nothing more than a carton of Bit-O-Honeys or an old Betty Grable film. But now, still looking at Ted Mack's "Original Amateur Hour," he felt the breakthrough was at hand. Excitedly, he dialed Roland Magruder's number.

When Roland answered, Barnett sang, "Good morning, Breakfast Clubbers, good morning to ya. We got up bright and early just to howdy-do ya."

"Unbelievable," said Roland, without much enthusiasm.

Roland and Barnett had formerly greeted each other with headlines from the *National Enquirer,* but one evening Roland had walked into a party and said, " 'Ripped His Heart Out; Stomped on It,' " and Barnett, realizing he could never hope to top that, had feverishly searched for new ways to open their conversations ever since.

"I think I've found the way to capture the heart of Rosalie Mondle," Barnett said.

Roland sighed and said, "Kid, if it's Cassius Clay quotes again, take an old pal's advice and forget it before you embarrass yourself."

"It's Ted Mack's 'Original Amateur Hour,' " Barnett said.

"Not Major Bowes?" asked Roland. He sounded surprised. "You must have heard Lester read his ode to Major Bowes."

Barnett hesitated for only a moment. "There are no tapes of the old Bowes shows," he said, hoping this was true. "But Ted Mack is on every Sunday, and, let me tell you, it's just too much."

"I'm awfully busy now, Barnett," Roland said. He was working on an anthology of *Daily News* editorials and often complained of the strain.

Barnett persisted, and Roland finally listened to his explanation of why Ted Mack's "Original Amateur Hour" was certainly Pop and probably Camp.

"You know, you might have something there," Roland finally said.

"Gloryosky, Zero!" whispered Barnett to himself. "I think this is it."

Barnett planned the campaign carefully. He spent three weeks cultivating an acquaintance who worked for a film magazine and could arrange with the network to show him all the old Ted Mack video tapes. When this had been set up, he spent days in the viewing room, patiently studying tap-dancers, saw-players, head-thumpers, and imitators of animals. He perfected his own imitation of Ted Mack and practiced night after night with his tape recorder until the voice that said "Round and round it goes and where it stops nobody knows" immediately conjured up a vision of Ted Mack smiling affably beside the Wheel of Fortune. He carefully picked his evening. The entire crowd was going to Roseland Dance City Sunday night and then to the home of Bernie and Greta Mohler to hear Randy Michaelman do his imitation of the Pete Smith Specialties. After half an hour of drinking Manischewitz Chablis at the Mohlers', Barnett thought he had worked up enough courage to approach Rosalie. She was, as usual, paying no attention to him, but she was alone except for Roland Magruder. They were standing in a corner, chatting about Busby Berkeley's finale for "Gold Diggers of 1933."

"Hello, Barnett," said Rosalie, when he walked over to join them. She had the mocking half smile that Roland Magruder had once compared to the look on Clark Kent's face when Lois Lane talked about the virility of Superman but that Barnett Frummer had always found merely terrifying.

"Are you going to the Dick Tracy serial at the Modern Museum next Sunday?" Roland asked Barnett. "I hear Pruneface gets his in this one."

"I always stay home on Sundays to watch Ted Mack's 'Original Amateur Hour,'" Barnett replied, trying to sound casual.

"To watch *who?*" asked Rosalie.

"Ted Mack," said Barnett. "He's fantastic."

"That does sound kind of incredible," said Rosalie. She seemed to be showing some interest.

"I happened to see a couple of ladies playing 'Buckle Down, Winsocki' on window shades on the show the other day," Barnett went on. "Also on Venetian blinds. They were androgynous as hell."

"Too much," Rosalie said.

"It's fantastically naïve," said Barnett. "Very pure, really."

"I don't think what happened today is anything to joke about, Barnett," said Roland, suddenly becoming very stern.

"What do you mean, 'What happened today'?" asked Barnett. He was puzzled; there had been nothing at all in his plan about this.

"You mean you didn't see this afternoon's show?" said Roland.

"As a matter of fact, I missed it today," Barnett said. Roland had been kind enough to tip him off to a hearing of old "Lorenzo Jones" tapes being held at the Ninety-second Street Y that afternoon, and Barnett had decided that the thoroughness of his previous research permitted him to miss the final program before the confrontation with Rosalie.

"As I understand it," Roland said, "Mack announced today that from now on he'll give a special prize every week for the act that gets the least votes compared to the amount of equipment used. I was shocked."

"The *least* votes!" Barnett exclaimed.

"As I understand it, the prize will go to the act that finishes last when you divide the number of votes by the pounds of paraphernalia, not counting tap shoes," said Roland. "I suppose he's calling it something like a 'Failed Seriousness Quotient.'"

"*Ted Mack* is doing this?"

"I think this kind of thing could spread until nothing in the culture has any value any more," said Roland. "Don't you think so, Barnett?"

"Yeah, it could spread," Barnett mumbled, walking toward the kitchen. As he reached the wine, he could hear Rosalie say, "Isn't Barnett just too much?"

"Not to be believed," said Roland as he took her arm and guided her toward the door. On their way down the hall, she looked up at him admiringly, and he smiled and sang her the opening song from Don McNeill's "Breakfast Club."

Lester Drentluss, a Jewish Boy from Baltimore, Attempts to Make It through the Summer of 1967

Although Lester Drentluss, the mildly promising New York editor, held a party celebrating Israel's military victory and modestly accepted congratulations at the door, he was not someone who had become militantly Jewish only when it became clear that the Israeli armies had crushed the combined might of the Arab world. Lester had detected a fashion for Jewishness in his own world several years before, when Yiddish words began to appear in the conversation of his firm's chief editor, Douglas Drake, a Methodist minister's son from Eau Claire, Wisconsin. "There's no use trying to sell books to the *goyim*," Drake had said one day as he announced his decision to devote 90 per cent of the firm's advertising budget to a historical novel based on the saga of the first Jewish frogman.

"But why would he put down his own majority group?" Lester asked later, when he had learned from Drake's secretary, an Irish girl from Queens, that *goyim* means gentiles.

The secretary shrugged. "Everybody's got his own *mishogas,*" she said.

Although Lester was Jewish, he felt left out. ("It means 'craziness,'" the secretary added impatiently, anxious to get back to her copy of *The Source.*) His family had been in Baltimore, Maryland, for five generations, and his parents were so militantly Americanized that he had once been spanked for doing an imitation of Al Jolson in *The Jazz Singer.* Whenever his mother heard anything that sounded as if it might be Yiddish, she immediately said, "Well, I'm sure I don't know what that means"—a habit that was so ingrained that she once blurted out "Well, I'm sure I don't know what that means" after a brother-in-law she suspected of overt Jewishness told her he wanted to keep a bit of gossip *"entre nous."*

At the first word of Yiddish from Douglas Drake, Lester decided to reappraise his own ethnic situation; Drake was known as a trend-spotter. Soon Lester began to spot some signs of a trend himself—a boom in Jewish novels here, a Jewish Lord Mayor of Dublin there. He noticed an increasing use of Jewish mothers by comedians and of Jewish advisers by politicians. Scotch-Irish professors seemed undisturbed about being included in the category of "Jewish intellectuals." The gentile movie stars who failed to convert to Judaism repented by donating their talents to Bonds for Israel benefits. The subway graffiti had begun to include phrases like "Medea Is a Yenta" and "Kafka Is a Kvetch." Lester's final decision came in February, 1965, while he was reading an article in *Life* magazine about Robert Lowell, the New England poet. "Do I feel left-out in a Jewish age?" Lowell was quoted as saying. "Not at all. Fortunately, I'm one-eighth Jewish myself, which I do feel is a saving grace." Lester decided that the day a Boston Lowell bragged about being Jewish was the day a Baltimore Drentluss ought to let it be known that he was at least eight times as Jewish as Robert Lowell.

That night, he tried out his Jewishness tentatively on Abigail Higgins, a willowy blonde on whom he had been trying things out tentatively for six months with little success. "I think it's rather ironic that America's Everyman might turn out to be Herzog instead of some *goy*," he said to Abigail as they had wine and gefilte fish at the apartment of Lemuel Scroggins, the Southern Populist poet.

"The Jewish sensibility is really rather unique," Abigail said.

"Thank you very much," Lester said, trying to shrug his shoulders in the manner of Menasha Skulnik. "Nice of you to say so."

Gradually, Lester began to tell self-deprecating stories about the quaintly domineering mother who had raised him on love and chicken soup with kreplach (his mother, in fact, had only tasted kreplach once, at the home of a poor relation, and had taken pains to compliment the host-

53

ess on the lightness of her won tons). He published a short literary-quarterly article called "The Schlemiel as Hero in American Literature." He complained often of heartburn.

Robert Lowell had been right; it was a Jewish world. At work, Lester's colleagues seemed to take a new interest in his opinions on which Jewish novel to publish each month. At the fashionable bagels-and-lox brunches given by Lemuel Scroggins on Sundays, Lester began to feel more a part of the conversation. Scroggins phoned to invite him almost every week—usually adding that he should "bring along that li'l' ole blond *shiksa* Abigail." Lester's acquaintances began to assume that Abigail was his to bring along; she often confided to the girls in the group that the most exciting men were "Mediterranean types." Lester also suspected that he was communicating better with Wash Jefferson, the group's favorite Negro. "Don't think I don't understand your suffering, Wash," he said to Jefferson just after the Selma march. "We've all been down that road."

"You sure are a sensitive mother," Jefferson said.

Lester's only problem was his parents, who decided to pay him a visit when his letters began to take on a disturbingly ethnic tone. "Well, I'm sure I don't know what that means," his mother had said after Lester called his gouging landlord a *goniff* while showing his parents through the apartment. "You certainly didn't pick up language like that at home, I can tell you that."

Lester's father, who had seemed calmer than his wife at

first, suddenly accused his son of learning Yiddish at Berlitz, an idea that had actually occurred to Lester at one point before he finally prevailed upon Douglas Drake's secretary to help him with his Yiddish during lunch hours.

"I thought you might like to see *Fiddler on the Roof* tonight," Lester said, trying to re-establish a friendly atmosphere as he passed his mother a drink and a plate of cocktail blintzes. "They say it manages to convey some of the tradition of humor and suffering that all of us carry from the ghetto."

"What ghetto!" his mother said. She began to cry.

"I'm surprised at you, talking to your mother like that," Mr. Drentluss said. "Don't the traditions of our people mean anything to you, Lester—five generations in Baltimore, a law firm full of gentiles? How can you flout your own heritage?"

"But people change in America," Lester said. "Frankly, Dad, the old traditions are mostly a lot of *mishogas*."

"I'm sure I don't know what that means," his mother said, between sobs. "I'm only thankful that your grandparents aren't alive to see this."

For his Israeli Victory Party, Lester had tried to rent Yonah Schimmel's Knishery, and then decided to settle for his own apartment. He and Abigail arranged a magnificent display of food; Lemuel Scroggins said it looked like "the Great Bar Mitzvah in the Sky."

"*Mazel tov,*" Douglas Drake said when he came in. "It's a great day, even though the Ringling Brothers–Barnum

& Bailey Tent Fire Disaster of 1944 has erupted in my chest."

"With me it's felt like the Coconut Grove fire since that lunch," Lester said. He and Drake often compared heartburn symptoms, and both were suffering from a huge lunch celebrating Lester's triumph in landing a blockbuster book that every publisher had been after—a first-person account by the only Jewish-American dentist to take part in the Sinai Campaign. Abigail, clinging to Lester's biceps, told Drake that the company should do a follow-up book on the tradition of ferocity in the Mediterranean fighting man. Lester shrugged.

Just three or four weeks after the Victory Party, during a period when Lester was in the habit of humming *"Havanagilah"* in the elevators, he was surprised and disturbed to read that an officer of the Student Nonviolent Coordinating Committee had made a speech complaining about Zionist aggression and "Jew storekeepers." Two or three Episcopal priests of Lester's acquaintance resigned from S.N.C.C. in protest, and some of his Jewish friends endorsed the statement and asked forgiveness. Lester was confused. A few days later, he overheard somebody at a Lemuel Scroggins brunch say that Jewish storekeepers in the ghetto were more at fault for the summer riots than anybody, with the possible exception of Jewish liberals. Lester thought at first that it might have been an isolated incident, but then Douglas Drake, with ominous enthusiasm, asked him to read the manuscript of a black nationalist book called *Can the Jews Atone for Everything on the Day of Atonement?* Moved by the manuscript, Lester phoned Wash Jefferson to apologize.

"I don't blame you," he said to Jefferson.

"Don't blame me for what, man?" Jefferson asked. "Did you get blackballed at one of those clubs I put you up for?"

"I don't blame you for hating me," Lester said.

"I don't hate you, Goldberg," Jefferson said.

"My name is Drentluss."

"You Jews sure are sensitive mothers," Jefferson said.

Lester stopped humming in the elevators. "I don't know what this storekeeper business has to do with you," his mother wrote him when she heard he was depressed. "Your people have been professional men for three generations." Lester was surprised to find himself slightly cheered up by his mother's letter; his relatives were innocent, and he himself could hardly be accused of exploiting the ghetto when he had never been there. A week later, his spirits dropped again when he was not included in a Scroggins brunch honoring some people who had participated in a seminar called "Black Power, the Third World and the Exploiters." Abigail went, and reported that Lemuel, who had formerly spoken of Negroes as "them poor downtrodden *schwartzas* in Alabama," was beginning to talk about "black people"—whether he was referring to his cleaning lady, Hazel M. Jones, or to Colonel Gamal Abdel Nasser.

One night, late in the summer, Douglas Drake, who no longer seemed to be suffering from heartburn, came to Lester's apartment to drop off a rush manuscript on the agonies of the Palestine refugees. As Drake walked in, Abigail looked up from a magazine article on the Israeli occupation of Old Jerusalem and asked Lester if he thought it was wise for non-Christians to have control over Christian shrines.

"I don't know much about it," Lester said.

"It's hard to understand why they won't at least give back the West Bank of the Jordan," Drake said. "After all that napalm they dropped on it, it can't be worth much anyway."

"They're a strange people," Lester said. "They surely are." He couldn't understand why Drake seemed to hold him personally responsible for what Jews did in Jordan; his family had been in Baltimore for five generations.

Abigail looked up from her magazine again. "I think Moshe Dayan might have too much *chutzpah* for his own good," she said.

Drake smiled at Lester knowingly.

Lester looked puzzled. *"Chutzpah?"* he said. "I don't think I know what that means."

Barnett Frummer
in Urban Crisis

"What do you think of Max Bergwort's latest?" Barnett Frummer asked the group at Randy Michaelman's one autumn evening. He was trying to sound casual, although his question was part of a plan that had included committing to memory all reviews of Maximillian Bergwort's recently published novel, *Mouthful of Angels,* testing literary observations on a tape recorder for casualness, and making certain that the conversation was launched at a time when Rosalie Mondle was near enough to be impressed at last by his wit and perception.

"Eight rooms rent-controlled on West End Avenue at a hundred and sixty has to be a good deal no matter what condition it's in," Elliot Nardling said.

Barnett looked at Elliot blankly. "Bergwort, as has often been noted, is, for better or worse, a writer with a point of view," he said slowly, continuing with his prepared text despite Elliot's puzzling remark.

"Does he have a river view?" Rosalie asked.

"Does he what?" Barnett said, looking around for some hint of what was going on.

"I think they're renting anything with a river view in those West End Avenue buildings as professional or semi-professional," Elliot said.

Barnett tried improvising slightly. "Bergwort is, of course, professional in his approach to the craft," he said, but he was beginning to believe that the conversation had slipped away from him. If he hadn't been certain that he was in the presence of sophisticated New Yorkers vitally engaged in communications, politics, and the arts, he could have sworn they were talking about apartments.

"I think there is a view," Douglas Drake said. "It's Plenet's old place—the one he got by getting the super's daughter into the Miss Subway contest."

"Talk about a fantastic deal!" Elliot said. "The place the Plenets have now is eleven huge rooms for one-twenty a month, counting utilities—on the second floor of a Chase Manhattan Bank branch. They can only go in and out during bank hours, of course, ten to three on weekdays, but you've never seen that much floor space."

Rosalie appeared to be only mildly impressed. "I didn't see you at the housewarming," Elliot said to her.

"It's hard for me to get away on a Tuesday morning," she said.

Barnett looked from face to face. He seemed to be moving physically from the center of the conversation; he was at least six feet from Rosalie already. Didn't anyone want to know about Bergwort's use of language? Wasn't anyone interested in how the surrealistic touches seemed to detract from rather than add to the over-all thrust of the book? Had he again become the master of the wrong subject? A few weeks before—having learned that the guest of honor at a dinner party to which both he and Rosalie were invited would be Hillary Blatt, the versatile Jewish-Jesuit ecumenist, anthropologist, gadfly, and father of three—Barnett had tried to prepare for the wide range of Blatt's interests by doing extensive research on comparative religion, international relations, astrology, radical politics, rock music, and field hockey. But at the dinner party nobody seemed to talk to Blatt about anything except his essays in *Beautiful Spot, The Magazine of Parking.*

"I suppose, in a sense, New York is a Jewish city the way Geneva was once a Calvinist city," Barnett had said as the hors d'oeuvres were passed around.

"Well, alternate-side-of-the-street parking regulations are suspended on Simchas Torah as well as on Rosh Hashonah and Yom Kippur, if that's what you mean," Blatt said. "But that is also true of Christmas, Good Friday, Washington's Birthday, and all snow emergencies."

Barnett concentrated for a while on his stuffed mushroom. He considered forgoing the question with which he had hoped to start a discussion of the United Nations. But if he didn't ask whether the existence of a world government organization for nearly a quarter of a century had really had any impact, what could he ask? He was confused enough without getting into astrology. Not asking, he realized, might mean that he would sit eight feet from Rosalie Mondle all evening staring silently at a stuffed mushroom. He asked.

"Two thousand cars with diplomatic plates are bound to have some effect on the parking situation throughout the city," Blatt said. "But I personally think that the 'Diplomatic Parking Only' signs rather than the additional cars constitute the larger problem. If anyone has a map . . ."

The host walked to the windows, pulled down a shade, and, finding that it had a parking map of Greenwich Village on it, tried two or three more shades until he came to one that showed parking possibilities in the United Nations area—with various colors indicating Alternate-Side-Parking, No Parking Anytime, Diplomatic Parking Only, No Parking Eight to Six, and Taxi Stands. The hostess passed Blatt a celery stalk, and he began to point out parking spots on the map, like an Air Force flight officer briefing his pilots. Barnett was stunned. Could there be a place in such a scene for a question about whether or not World Peace Through World Law was a viable concept in the face of competing megapowers? Then Rosalie seemed about to say something, and Barnett allowed himself to hope that the conversation might be returned to a subject for which he had done some preparation. "There's an interesting corollary to your theory about bus stops on First Avenue," Rosalie said. She stood up, walked to the window shade, and turned to the hostess. "Do you happen to have an extra celery stalk?" she asked.

"Overcope," Roland Magruder explained when Barnett drove out to see him a few days after the apartment discussion. Roland, who was working on a study called "Efforts of Middle-Class White Over-achievers to Deal with the Manhattan Environment," was temporarily staying with a cousin in Metuchen, New Jersey. "Rosalie has fallen in with that overcope crowd."

"But I thought only suburban businessmen talked about real estate," Barnett said, after asking Roland if he happened to be interested in listening to a few casual observations on the works of Maximillian Bergwort.

"Only suburban businessmen talk about books," Roland said. "My study indicates that Manhattan writers talk more about real estate than any other occupational group, although they are slightly behind Wall Street lawyers and Madison Avenue advertising executives in talking about which schools to send their children to, and they are a poor fifth in discussing the problems of maids, nurses, and *au pair* girls."

"But these are people vitally engaged in communications, politics, and the arts, interested in how the surrealistic touches detracted from rather than added to the book, concerned with whether or not World Peace Through World Law is a viable concept in the face of competing megapowers," Barnett said. "Aren't they?"

"Why do you think Rosalie admires Douglas Drake?" Roland asked.

"Because he's one of the top editors at Ginsberg and Gilbert?" Barnett said, without conviction.

"Wrong again," Roland said. "It's because Douglas Drake knows midtown Manhattan so well that once, on a rainy day, he managed to walk from Forty-Third Street to Fifty-Eighth Street without going out of doors—although, as it happened, he was on his way to Fourteenth Street at the time."

"Amazing!" Barnett said.

"Pure overcope," Roland said, with some disdain, and went back to reading the evening edition of the Metuchen *News-Record*.

As he crisscrossed his neighborhood that evening vainly looking for a parking spot, Barnett began to face a depressing fact: what impressed Rosalie Mondle was ability to cope with a city in which he had always considered it a triumph just to maintain existence. For years, the only way he had ever been able to find his way anyplace on the subway was to write his destination under a note that said "I Am a Hungarian Freedom Fighter" and present it wordlessly to anyone in uniform—a practice he discontinued after he handed the note to a Transit Authority patrolman named Zoltan Scakrasnye, who arrested him on the charge of impersonating a Magyar. There was a bus that stopped right across the street from his apartment house, but Barnett had never been able to find out where it came from.

And the more he thought about what Roland had said, the clearer it became that Randy Michaelman, the up-and-coming advertising man, was known not for his brilliant penetration of the sub-teen water-softener market but for his coolness in placing his landlord under citizen's arrest one December when the heat in his apartment dropped below the statutory minimum of sixty-eight degrees. He remembered that Howard Fox—who, in Barnett's mind, had always been the model of the sophisticated, with-it free-lance writer—had done his latest article on how the rich and mighty go about choosing a dentist in Manhattan. And where did that leave him, he thought, as he creased his fender rushing into a spot that an Oldsmobile had suddenly vacated. He looked out the window. In front of a fireplug, that's where.

Resolutely, Barnett began to cope. He vowed that if Rosalie Mondle was impressed with people who were skilled on the subway and knowledgeable about cheap little restaurants and cunning about getting theater tickets, he would become skilled and knowledgeable and cunning —or get lost trying. He went down into the subway without his Freedom Fighter card, spent hours trying to find imaginative short-cuts to any place he had any reason to suspect that Rosalie might ever want to go, and somehow ended up every time at Queens Plaza—a place he had no reason to suspect that Rosalie might ever want to go, since he hadn't been aware of its existence. With three weeks of research and a five-dollar-and-eighty-five-cent taxi ride, he was able to discover an Eastern European sailors' hangout near the Brooklyn docks where Latvian shaslik could be obtained for a dollar seventy-five, with choice of appetizer —and to discover further that Latvian shaslik caused him to break out in a painful rash. In December, only two months after his coping effort began, he was able to tell a gathering at Randy Michaelman's that he was planning to see a sold-out Broadway play by casually walking up to the box office on Christmas Eve—only to discover that a half-dozen people at Randy Michaelman's had seen the play two months before by casually walking up to the box office on Kol Nidre.

Barnett pressed on. He managed to learn where the bus that stopped across from his apartment building came from (Queens Plaza). One February evening at Randy Michaelman's, he seemed to draw mild approval by mentioning a modest but solidly researched essay he had written on where to find men's rooms in midtown, and by outlining to everyone his method of avoiding taxi-driver monologues —an extension of his Freedom Fighter device in which he handed the driver a card that had on it his destination above the words "I Am Deaf," and then sank woodenly into the back seat. At the same party, in a discussion he had started about methods of forcing Macy's to deliver merchandise within a month or two of the promised date —a discussion held within earshot of Rosalie Mondle— Barnett said, "I've found that wiring the chief counsel of the corporation your intention to go to small-claims court will almost always get delivery within a week."

"Yes, I suppose the old small-claims device is still all

right if you're in no hurry," Myrna Nardling said. "But every time I've threatened to chain myself to the front door of the Thirty-Fourth Street store, delivery has come the same day."

Barnett realized that he could never match the breadth of experience of married couples like Myrna and Elliot Nardling, who had so many more facets of the city to cope with. How, for instance, could he compare schemes by which Haitian maids and Scandinavian *au pair* girls were smuggled past immigration officials? He had no maid or *au pair* girl—merely a West Indian cleaning woman who came in one day every other week to terrify him with stories about how the regularity of her fierce cleaning was the only thing preventing the occupation of his apartment by the Cockroach Army, and to frustrate him by hiding his kitchen utensils in fiendishly logical places. He had to stand by silently while Bernie and Greta Mohler bragged to Rosalie about the full-time maid they had imported from the New Hebrides to work for seven dollars a month. (According to Bernie, there were some communications problems brought on by the fact that she spoke a language spoken by only one other person in the metropolitan area —her cousin, a professional housebreaker—but it also meant that, being unable to communicate with other maids, she still hadn't heard about days off.) All Barnett could do was nod his head in a way that he hoped gave the impression of understanding and experience when Myrna Nardling told how she and Elliot had finally managed to get their six-year-old daughter accepted at a fashionable and overapplied-to progressive school by formally declaring her a Negro. Barnett didn't have a six-year-old daughter of any race. He didn't even have a wife. It was becoming more and more difficult for him to hold out any hope that he would ever have Rosalie.

Toward the end of March—at a time when Barnett was so preoccupied with his failure to cope that he sometimes got lost on the way *to* the subway—he was suddenly presented with the kind of accidental good fortune that he had long ago decided was reserved only for the Mohlers and Nardlings of the world. A distant cousin who worked in the administration of Medicare benefits happened to learn of an extraordinary apartment that was about to become available at the death of an elderly widow—eleven rooms at Seventieth and Fifth Avenue overlooking Central Park for eighty-seven fifty a month rent-controlled. ("Terrace. Twenty-four-hour doorman and elevator man," Barnett's cousin went on, after Barnett had already said that he would do anything, including attending the next family reunion at Rehoboth Beach, Delaware, for the apartment. "Wired for air-conditioning. Beautifully maintained. The people who work in the building refuse to accept Christmas gratuities from the tenants, believing that pride and satisfaction in service properly rendered is enough reward for anyone. . . .") Remarkably, the lease on the apartment Barnett was living in was about to expire. As he outlined his plan to Roland Magruder, he intended to move into the new place immediately, so he could mention it casually within Rosalie's hearing at Randy Michaelman's gathering on the following Friday. It was an exceptionally warm March day, and Barnett had decided that the relaxation of the drive to Metuchen and the opportunity to tell Roland of his triumph would justify the anxiety involved in moving his car with the knowledge that he would probably be unable to find another spot when he returned.

"You're not coping very well," Roland said. "The thing to do is not to move in yourself but to offer it casually to anyone who's interested—including Rosalie. That implies you have a better one."

Barnett was sorry not to be able to live in the Fifth Avenue apartment himself. For three years, he had been occupying a studio apartment in a hideously ugly new building with exorbitant rents and wafer-thin walls, and he was often kept up at night by the card-shuffling of an insomniac solitaire fanatic who lived two floors below him. But he would have been willing to live in the street in order to impress Rosalie Mondle with his ability to find a place to live; he signed a new three-year lease and hoped he could convince himself that card-shuffling was the kind of noise that lulled a person to sleep.

At Randy Michaelman's that Friday, he sounded as casual as he had sounded in rehearsal. "I don't suppose anyone would be interested in eleven rooms for eighty-seven fifty," he said, as soon as he had manuevered to within ten feet of Rosalie.

"In the Vineyard or East Hampton?" Elliot Nardling asked.

Barnett found himself looking blankly at Elliot again. "East Hampton is ruined," Randy Michaelman said. "So's the Vineyard," Rosalie said. "Every place is ruined."

"Fifth Avenue," Barnett said. "In the seventies." But nobody seemed to hear him. Rosalie was listing for Elliot all of the summer places she considered ruined, and Randy and Douglas Drake were arguing about whether the best route to Quogue was cutting down from the Long Island Expressway or going straight out the Southern State Parkway from the Belt.

"Have you thought about Mexico?" Elliot was asking Rosalie. "We were there years ago, of course. It's probably ruined."

"Mexico is ruined," Rosalie said.

"At least it has the ruins," Elliot said.

"Twenty-four-hour doorman," Barnett mumbled. "Also elevator man."

"The ruins are ruined," Rosalie said.

"A view of the park," Barnett said, half to himself, as he drifted farther and farther from Rosalie. "Recently rewired for air-conditioning. Terrace. Near the zoo." Nobody was listening. Barnett decided to go home. He walked alone to the subway. Even if he got lost and ended up at Queens Plaza, he thought, he could always take a bus.

Barnett Frummer
Turns Black with Desire

"I just found out today that a black man invented one of the parts absolutely essential to the air brake," Rosalie Mondle said loudly. "I think it's shocking that white Americans simply weren't told about that. Don't you?"

They were gathered at the apartment of Randy Michaelman, an indefatigable amateur pianist, and they had to speak loudly to be heard over the noise of Randy playing his own adaptation of an Ibo war chant.

"Yes, where would we all be without the air brake?" Lester Drentluss said, nodding his head vigorously.

Standing at the edge of the group, Barnett Frummer wanted to add something, but all he could think of to say was "It's the only thing stopping us," and he was afraid that wouldn't be appropriate.

"Tell us whites that a black man wrote 'Eugene Onegin' and we're shocked out of our precious skins!" Marshall Slovin said.

Barnett wondered why he could never think of anything to say when Rosalie Mondle was in the room. "How about 'Carry Me Back to Ole Virginny?'" he finally blurted out. Across the room, Randy Michaelman looked momentarily puzzled, and then shrugged and began to play "Carry Me Back to Ole Virginny."

"No! No!" Barnett said, when everybody turned to stare at Randy. "I meant that a black man wrote 'Carry Me Back to Ole Virginny.' James A. Bland. He also wrote 'Oh, Dem Golden Slippers.'"

"And also 'The Amos and Andy Show?'" Rosalie said sarcastically.

"No, I think 'In the Evening by the Moonlight' was his only other well-known work," Barnett said, but by the way Rosalie glared at him he realized he had fumbled again.

When the subject of race had first become popular at Randy Michaelman's parties, around 1963, Barnett was reasonably certain that if he attended the March on Washington he would be marching in step with (even if not precisely at the side of) Rosalie Mondle—although, as it turned out, he missed the March on Washington, having been arrested for speeding on the New Jersey Turnpike by a vicious-looking Negro state trooper. Rosalie had definitely been in Washington for the March; Barnett later heard her express outrage at Rolly Rawlings for sending three dozen picnic lunches from the Brasserie to members of the Moss Point, Mississippi, N.A.A.C.P. Youth Council. "How could she bring herself to trade there after the way the French tortured an oppressed majority in Algeria?" Rosalie had said.

For some time after the March, Barnett could be certain of Rosalie's presence at parties where whites gathered to be castigated by some prominent Negro for their part in four hundred years of rape and genocide, but he couldn't seem to get invited himself. "I can't understand it," he told Roland Magruder. "I don't like to blow my own horn, but I do think I'm as guilty as anybody."

Barnett could, of course, go to the public meetings that Rosalie was likely to attend, but he found them nerve-wracking: Rosalie's views on race advanced so quickly that Barnett never knew whether to go to a meeting prepared to applaud every speaker vehemently or to picket all of them as racists. After a while, he couldn't even count on Rosalie's presence at public meetings. One night, he attended a benefit concert given by "Friends of the N.A.A.C.P.," only to discover the next morning that Rosalie had spent the evening denouncing the N.A.A.C.P. at a discothèque benefit called "An Evening of Frugging for the Student Nonviolent Coordinating Committee." He made it a point to attend the next S.N.C.C. benefit, but someone there told him that Rosalie was attending an oud recital held to raise bail for some members of the Black Vengeance Patrol.

Barnett did occasionally see Rosalie at Randy Michaelman's, but he was beginning to feel that by the time he did enough research to be able to present a confident speech in support of one of Rosalie's positions, she was bound to be militantly committed to the opposite view. After he heard Rosalie rage at the de facto segregation caused by a slavish adherence to neighborhood schools, Barnett made himself a lay expert on the subject—taking care to sit near a Negro, or at least a Puerto Rican, whenever he went to the library—and when he considered himself just about ready to offer a distinguished explanation of just why the concept of neighborhood schools was not really an integral part of American educational history, he heard Rosalie say that only a racist would deny that people in black neighborhoods have the right to run their own schools for their own children. On the night Barnett felt prepared to leap into the conversation with a speech about the success of a multiracial society in Hawaii and the findings of a renowned ecologist that the birds of the air and the beasts of the field actually *do* go around in integrated groups, Rosalie captivated the guests at Randy Michaelman's by reciting a poem entitled "Black Panthers Must Stalk with Black Panthers; Let White Buzzards Keep to Their Flock." At one point, Barnett felt pretty knowledgeable about an insurance company's project to create jobs for Negroes outside the ghettos, and at that point Rosalie let it be known that the only economic answer was to provide investment capital for Negroes inside Harlem. Barnett immediately began looking into investment possibilities, and finally, months later, he was able to announce at Randy Michaelman's that he had joined a group of young white businessmen who had gathered together to back a Negro clothes designer and a Harlem dress store in a new line of maternity clothes called "Mother Jumpers."

"How does it feel to be a neocolonialist?" Rosalie said.

"It's impossible to keep up," Barnett said to Roland Magruder one night. "Whenever I was about to quote Martin Luther King, she was quoting Malcolm X. When I got the people in my office to sign a resolution against the poll tax, she had already persuaded her friend Linda Golbhelder to start a Crispus Attucks Chapter of Hadassah in Larchmont. The other night, I was about to tell her about my Frederick Douglass poster when I noticed that she was wearing a button with a picture of Menelik II of Ethiopia. I don't know where to go from here."

"Why don't you invite her over for dinner?" Roland asked.

"I don't think this is a time for joking," Barnett said. "Why should she come to my house for dinner?"

"I think she'd come if you told her you were having a bunch of militant spades," Roland said. Roland was considered by far the most sophisticated of Barnett's acquaintances in racial matters, having freed himself from white middle-class guilt to the extent of being able to refer to Negroes by what Rosalie had formerly referred to contemptuously as "derogatory racial appellations." Roland had, in fact, suggested that Barnett do the same if he wanted to impress Rosalie, but Barnett couldn't bring himself to use the words—although once, desperate to be noticed, he had mumbled something about "darkies," but too softly for anybody to hear.

Barnett decided to follow Roland's advice. He turned for help to his only Negro friend, Wash Jefferson, an advertising man he had met in the Army. "I don't know what you see in that girl," Wash said, when Barnett presented him with the plan. "She's always coming up to me at parties and saying, 'Why don't we rap for a while, baby?' I think anyone who uses 'baby' to address anyone over the age of two should be put in the stocks. Surely you're not impressed just because she has the only natural-blond Afro haircut on East Seventy-Fourth Street?"

Barnett didn't know how to explain his feeling for Rosalie. What could he say, except that he was willing to sit through a four-hour debate on open-housing ordinances just for the opportunity to catch a glimpse of her in her black beret? There was no way to describe what he felt as he stood in the rain in front of the school-board building and watched her pass up and down with a placard saying "Go Back Where You Came From, Honkies!"

"Oh, what the hell," Wash finally said, as Barnett looked more and more dejected. "I'm probably just overreacting to that time she lectured me for not knowing more about the contribution of the Negro cowboy to the development of the Southwest. I'll do it."

Within a few weeks, Wash had managed to collect dinner commitments from a biographer of Marcus Garvey, two young Negroes under indictment for criminal anarchy, a Liberian accountant who was also a poet, and the cousin of the first Negro Lincoln-Mercury dealer in New Jersey. Barnett planned to have the dinner catered by an Upper East Side soul-food restaurant. That left only the problem of how to ask Rosalie. At first, Barnett thought he might say casually, "I'm having a few people who happen to be Negro over for dinner next week," but then he remembered that Rosalie despised people who said "happen to be Negro"—as well as people who said "Negro." He thought it would be better to say "black." How about, "Say, Rosalie, I'm having a few black cats over for dinner?" But "black cats" sounded ambiguous. He still was not sure of his approach when he went to Randy Michaelman's next party in hopes of being able to put his invitation to Rosalie.

"I'm going to ask her tonight," he said to Marshall Slovin, the first person he saw as he walked in the door.

"Ask who what?" Marshall said.

"Ask Rosalie to dinner with some militant colored people," Barnett said.

"Haven't you heard?" Marshall said. "Rosalie just fired her Negro maid for being willing to work for a white. And she cut Wash Jefferson dead on the street this afternoon. She says that any black man who has no more self-respect than to talk to a honky woman is not worth talking to."

Barnett had a drink with Wash the next night. "I probably wouldn't have had the nerve to ask her anyway," Barnett said.

"Forget about her," Wash said. "Let me tell you about some of the more bizarre contributions that Negro cowboys made to the development of the Southwest."

"Actually, I really don't think it's that bad for you to talk to me," Barnett said. "Although naturally I would understand perfectly if you preferred not to."

"As a matter of fact, I'm so filled with self-loathing I can only stand to be around someone as guilt-ridden as you," Wash said.

Barnett knew he would have trouble making the adjustment from being ashamed of having only one Negro friend to being ashamed of having a Negro friend, and he and Wash decided to continue to have a few drinks together regularly—although Barnett planned to have the drinks in bars where there was no chance of being seen by anyone who knew Rosalie Mondle. There was no danger of being seen by Rosalie herself. Barnett had learned from Marshall Slovin that Rosalie, as a gesture of further support to the black struggle, no longer entered bars that served Negroes.

Marshall Slovin, the Borderline Literary Figure, Attempts to Make It All the Way

Marshall Slovin, the borderline literary figure, had been staring at the blank piece of paper in his typewriter for forty minutes. Finally, he ripped it out, crumpled it into a ball, and hurled it across the room. Sixteen days had passed since he had begun wrestling with his latest project—naming the three books he had enjoyed most during the year for a Christmas issue of *The Bookreader Fortnightly*. The request from the *Fortnightly* had at first seemed to him the final seal on his literary success; now he almost wished it had never come. He hadn't worked so hard on anything since the final agonizing days of completing his one novel, *A Pride of Cows*, when he had spent three weeks trying to decide whom to dedicate it to—a decision he eventually made in favor of thirty-one New York literary figures. He remembered the novel with a shudder.

By chance, it had been published during a brief period when the editor of the country's most influential book-review section would not permit a book to be reviewed by anyone who was personally acquainted with the author, and it had proved impossible to find a book reviewer in New York who was not personally acquainted with Marshall Slovin. The review had been assigned to a retired historian in Murdo, South Dakota, who normally specialized in reviewing books about Plains Indians, and it was eventually lost in the mails.

He had come a long way just to be stumped by the Christmas issue of *The Bookreader Fortnightly,* Slovin thought, as he grimly rolled another piece of paper into the carriage of his typewriter. He well remembered the days when he had to scramble to catch up with the literary taste others were making. Not many years before, in the summer of 1964, he had spent hundreds of hours in second-hand book stores until he found an old copy of *Lord of the Flies* that he could inscribe to his wife "From Marshall to Madeline, here's a sleeper that might interest you, Christmas 1959" and discreetly slip into their bookcase. Now he was being recognized, occasionally, as a tastemaker himself. Not because of *Cows*—which, lacking reviews, had sold only three hundred and twenty-eight copies—but because of a brutal schedule of reviewing books, attending parties, participating in demonstrations, chairing forums, and organizing volleyball games. With a brilliant *Fortnightly* list, he could forever put behind him those desperate days when he used to lurk around the beach at Amagansett for hours every summer weekend on the slim hope that the child of an important critic might lose a beachball or be swept out to sea in his direction and a grateful parent might invite him to a literary cocktail party. He looked down at the paper in his typewriter again, and began to type. *"War and Peace,"* he wrote.

"What have you written?" his wife, Madeline, shouted from the kitchen, where she was preparing a pot roast and a letter to the *New York Review of Books*.

"War and Peace," Marshall said. "It's brilliant! The implication is that I've read everything ever written and this year I started all over again."

"That's just dandy," Madeline said. "Irving Zentman has listed *War and Peace, Huckleberry Finn,* and the St. James version of the Bible every year since the *Fortnightly* began running the list; everybody considers *War and Peace* Irving Zentman's book; and if you list *War and Peace* you will never be assigned another *Bensonhurst Quarterly* review by Irving Zentman as long as he is the editor of the *Bensonhurst Quarterly*. Otherwise, it's a brilliant idea."

Marshall ripped out the paper, crumpled it into a ball, and hurled it across the room.

"Emmanuel Murray is naming a biography of St. Francis of Assisi as the book he enjoyed most," Madeline said.

"Manny Murray the pornographer!" Marshall shouted. "What the hell is *he* doing reading a biography of St. Francis of Assisi?"

"I understand that's the whole point," Madeline said. "He lists something totally unlikely in order to demonstrate the fantastic variety of his intellectual curiosity."

"Maybe I should list the Department of Agriculture pamphlet on spring wheat," Marshall said, sarcastically, but with a hint of consideration in his voice.

"You can if you want to appear derivative," Madeline said. "I understand Murray is using that one too. Also an epic poem on the founding of Lake Wales, Florida. And he's before you in the alphabet."

Four days later, still not having written a single title, Marshall was so dejected that only a strict policy of attending all literary gatherings prevented him from skipping Sunday lox-and-bagel brunch at the apartment of Lemuel Scroggins. The absolute deadline at the *Fortnightly* was the following morning, and every effort at the list had failed. Obscure books of poetry had become famous just as he was about to discover them. A friend in a publishing house, Lester Drentluss, had tipped him off to a totally unknown underground novel—*Lunchtime Leather,* by a homosexual jockey named Christopher Crown—but after reading it Marshall was afraid that it was so far underground it might never emerge. Abstruse foreign policy analyses that he was planning to say he had enjoyed in manuscript had turned out to be too abstruse to be published. Marshall hesitated as he reached for his Sunday tweed. He prided himself on being a person who could control the creative drive well enough to attend any necessary social functions, but he had become possessed by the *Fortnightly* list.

"I hope Marcel Katz is there," Madeline was saying, as

she adjusted her pants suit in the mirror. "I hear he's having a big party during the National Book Awards presentation this year for everybody who walks out."

Marshall wanted desperately to be invited to the Katz party; one year, he and Madeline had walked out of the presentation in order to protest the war in Vietnam and had wandered around for the rest of the evening with no place to go. But he realized that he had nothing but envy and loathing in his heart for Marcel Katz. For ten years, Katz had named only titles in foreign languages; in fact, he had refused to participate in the *Fortnightly* listing until the year the editors could assure him that they had obtained printing facilities that made it possible to set Cyrillic type.

"I hear those impressive foreign titles he listed last year turned out to be two Lithuanian sex novels and the guide to Addis Ababa," Marshall muttered, while knotting his red woolly tie. He thought of asking Irving Zentman for help—with his own choices settled permanently, Irving might be in a position to pass on a tip to a friend—but he was reluctant to ask Irving for a favor after having left him out of the *Cows* dedication. He tried to remember why Irving had not been included. He could remember telling Madeline that he was thinking of having Ferd and Ethyl Davidson.

"Ferd and Ethyl Davidson!" Madeline had shouted. "After that piece of dime-store jewelry they gave our Linda for her graduation! The only volume I'd dedicate to them is a book of S&H Green Stamps."

"Ferd had me," Marshall said, somewhat defensively.
"To that party with the pretzels and cheese-dip?" Madeline said.

"No, for the dedication of his last novel," Marshall said.

"Anyone in the dedication to that horror should have requested a pseudonym," Madeline said. "Also, the people in that dedication outnumbered the people who bought the book. With his big book, if you'll remember, it was just Irving Zentman."

"Maybe I should have Irving."

"If you have Jack McHugh you can't have Irving," Madeline reminded him. "Jack has hated Irving ever since that day Irving didn't choose him for softball in East Hampton, and Jack had you listed in the top line of the Peace Ad in the *Times*. He's your biggest booster, Marshall."

Now, as he thought of that conversation, Marshall could recall perfectly the huge chart he had kept above his desk in those days—the kind of chart that many novelists use to keep track of their characters. The people who could profitably be included in his dedication had all been on the chart—connected by dotted lines to show book-reviewing connections, red lines to indicate hostilities—and, with some regret, he remembered taking down the chart and crossing out the name of Irving Zentman. It might have been a mistake. These were the decisions that a literary figure had to make.

The first person the Slovins saw at the apartment of Lemuel Scroggins was a smirking Manny Murray, secure in the biography of St. Francis of Assisi, the Department of Agriculture pamphlet on spring wheat, and the epic poem on the founding of Lake Wales, Florida. Murray was talking to Max Bergwort, who also looked maddeningly calm. Every year, Bergwort merely listed three more picaresque novels. The previous year he had listed *Glug, Poornk,* and *Sludge.* The year before that, he had said that the three books he most enjoyed were *Blomp, Sturdge,* and *Fremck.* "I wouldn't be surprised if he named *Snap, Crackle,* and *Pop* this year," Marshall whispered to Madeline as they went over to test the undergroundness of Christopher Crown's *Lunchtime Leather* on Murray and Bergwort.

"I think Crown's a bit overrated," Marshall said casually, after a few minutes of conversation.

"In a way, I suppose he is," Murray said, in a way that didn't indicate to Marshall whether Murray had ever heard of Christopher Crown.

"No doubt," Bergwort said. "I read in the trade papers that *Leather* has been bought by Otto Preminger or somebody for a major motion picture. It's not half the novel *Blurnt* is."

Lester Drentluss, discovered near the lox-and-bagel table by Marshall a few minutes later, was apologetic about having recommended an underground novel that had already been unearthed. "I have an even better title for you," he told Marshall. "Have you considered *Kick Cultures and Throw Cultures?*"

"Well, naturally, I've considered it," Marshall said, trying to remember if he had ever heard of *Kick Cultures and Throw Cultures*. Then he remembered a brief review of it that his review-clipping service had sent him from the *Wyoming Quarterly*. It was the twelve-hundred-page master work of Konrad Ludwig, the M.I.T. geopsychiatrist, expounding his theory that countries could be categorized sociologically according to whether the predominant game in their culture required skill in throwing (e.g., baseball) or kicking (e.g., soccer football)—a difference that, according to Ludwig, was the real explanation of such disparate phenomena as tensions in the N.A.T.O. Alliance, the *entente* between Albania and China, and the gassy quality of English beer. Drentluss piled some cream cheese on his bagel, and, in a voice barely above a whisper, told Marshall that an obscure journal of Eastern European affairs was about to disclose that *Kick Cultures and Throw Cultures* was the favorite book of the Chairman of the Soviet Council of Ministers, the cornerstone of Russian policy toward the West, and therefore a necessity for any foreign policy expert's understanding of the Russians.

It took Slovin only a couple of minutes to locate Boris Blisnyarik, the Russian emigré foreign policy expert and social critic, who was sitting alone in a corner, wolfing down some smoked whitefish. "Mildly interesting," Blisnyarik said, when Marshall told him cryptically that a certain book would soon be revealed as the source of the Soviet view of the West. Then Blisnyarik sat silently for a while, staring at his remaining whitefish. "I have myself lately been reading an interesting book—a manuscript, really," he finally said. "I understand it will be accepted as the best of the ghetto-school books—the story of a young man who went into the Detroit school system to free the spirit of ghetto students, permitted his students to free their spirits in whatever way they wanted, accomplished extraordinary feats of spirit-freeing during the week he taught, and wrote of his experiences eloquently before succumbing to his injuries. I was thinking of including it on my *Fortnightly* list, but in a way it's not really in my field."

"Throw in a cult novel and you've got a deal," Marshall said.

When they got home that night, Marshall went immediately to the typewriter and wrote down the two titles he had received from Blisnyarik in exchange for *Kick Cultures and Throw Cultures*—the ghetto-school book, *Blacks Bored,* and the cult novel, *Grass in Mourning.* "That's dandy," Madeline said, when Marshall showed her the list. "I don't suppose you'll mind being the only person on the page with only two titles."

Marshall had forgotten about a third title. He went back and rolled the sheet into the typewriter. He needed a sleeper, a book that nobody had noticed. For thirty minutes, he sat silently at the typewriter. Then, his face brightened, and he typed one more title—*A Pride of Cows,* a novel by Marshall Slovin.

Barnett Frummer
Hears a Familiar Ring

Barnett Frummer was having one of his recurring dreams about not having enough dreams. A voice was explaining to him that everyone dreams approximately two hours each night, rearranging the experiences that the unconscious considers important, and Barnett was trying to explain to the voice that he just didn't have enough experiences to produce two hours of dreaming a night. Barnett could not seem to make the voice understand that the only experiences his unconscious or his conscious considered important were experiences involving Rosalie Mondle, and that he didn't see her often enough to account for more than five or ten minutes' worth of dreaming a month. After a while, the voice materialized into a stiff, pedantic little man, who sat in a straight chair next to Barnett's bed and rang a bell in Barnett's ear to prove he was dreaming. On the fifth or sixth ring, Barnett finally freed one hand from the bedcovers, fumbled for the telephone, and then paused to summon enough clarity of thought to say hello.

"Good morning," said a loud, metallic female voice on the other end of the wire. "U.S. Weather Bureau forecast for New York City. Eight a.m. Central Park readings: temperature sixty-four degrees, humidity seventy-four per cent, barometer two-nine-point-six-two and falling. Light rain and mist this morning, changing to—"

"Who asked?" said Barnett, finally able to speak. "Nobody asked you." He wrestled the receiver back into the cradle, turned over, and went back to sleep. When he woke up, two hours later, he thought the phone call must have been part of his dream. The dreams he did have about Rosalie often concerned phone calls. Once, he dreamed that Rosalie, whose telephone voice he had yearned in vain to hear, had phoned him long distance from some place like Paraguay, and all he could do was ask for her area code. "I want to speak to you, Barnett," she kept saying, trying to be heard over the babbling of the operator, who was speaking a language that was not quite Spanish. "I'm going to talk to you. I remember your name"—all the things he had waited so long to hear. Barnett had often spent hours musing about what he would say if Rosalie ever phoned him —he knew *he* would never work up the nerve to phone *her*—but in the dream he refused to engage in conversation. "I must have your area code, Madam," he kept saying. "This call cannot be completed without your area code."

He was thinking about that dream, shuddering now and then, when the telephone rang again. ". . . clear and mild late tonight and early Monday, followed by increasing cloudiness," the voice said. "Rain developing late in the day or at night . . ."

"I didn't call you," Barnett said. "I'm not planning to leave my apartment today."

". . . highest both days in the low eighties. Lowest to-night in the low seventies. Precipitation probability: to-day twenty-five per cent, increasing to fifty per cent early tonight and tomorrow. . . ."

Barnett hung up. Then he remained very still for a while. It was true that he phoned WE 6-1212 occasionally to learn the weather, but he didn't think he called any more often than anyone else. Or did he? People who char-coal-broiled steaks or organized picket lines must call con-stantly. Why pick him to call back? Was the telephone company trying to tell him something? It was true that under the prodding of some militant friends he had refused to accept 533-7257 as his new telephone number and had insisted on calling it JEhovah 3-7257. But the first time he tried to phone his apartment from out of town—he did that occasionally so the people in the next apartment would know they were living next door to someone who got his share of telephone calls—the operator had accepted his version of the exchange without argument and then dialed JEhovah as GE, connecting him to a man who cursed at him in Ukrainian. After that, he went back to 533. It was a minor incident, though, and he couldn't imagine that it could cause calls from the Weather Bureau. Finally, he picked up the telephone and dialed the home of his friends, Bernie and Greta Mohler. "Do you ever call the weather girl at WE 6-1212?" he asked when Bernie answered the phone.

"I was just about to call her, as a matter of fact," Bernie said. "You don't happen to know the precipitation probability, do you? We're planning to frolic in our neighborhood vestpocket park today."

"Twenty-five per cent, increasing to fifty per cent early tonight and tomorrow," Barnett said.

"Thanks very much," said Mohler.

"Bernie, *she* called *me!*" Barnett said.

"Right, Barnett. Look, sorry we have to run. Greta's waiting at the door. I'll phone you tomorrow."

"Sure, Bernie," Barnett said. "It's probably just something wrong with the phone, or something."

Mohler hung up the phone and fell back into his chair laughing. His wife, Greta, looked very serious. "I did not give you that tape recorder so you could torment your friends," she said. "Also, I'll bet tape recording a phone conversation without producing a beep is illegal in this state. Not to speak of childish."

"Greta," Bernie said, "how would the recorded voice of the weather girl know whether I was making a beep or not?"

"Poor Barnett would know it when you called up and played it back to him."

"Barnett happens to be a personal friend of mine," Bernie said.

"Well, I think it's just awful," said Greta. "What did he say?"

Bernie and Greta received another call from Barnett three nights later. Barnett sounded agitated. " 'My Little Chickadee' and 'The Bank Dick' are playing the R.K.O. 86th," he said to Bernie.

"I didn't know the chain nabes were showing the oldies," Mohler said. "That's very interesting. What else is new, Barnett?"

" 'My Little Chickadee' is shown at five-twenty-four, eight-oh-five, and ten-forty-six," Barnett said. " 'The Bank Dick' goes on a six-forty and nine-twenty-one."

"Thanks very much," said Bernie. "But we thought we'd stay in tonight."

"If you would like further information, please call Atwater 9-8900," Barnett said.

"I'm not even sure I want the information I already have," said Bernie.

"They called me up and told me all this," Barnett said.

"Who called you up?"

"The voice from R.K.O. 86th Street," Barnett said.

"Why would they call you?" Bernie asked.

"I don't know," said Barnett. "W. C. Fields I've always been able to take or leave."

"Maybe you should call the phone company."

"I better call them before they call me," Barnett said.

But after thinking it over for a few days, Barnett could not bring himself to call the telephone company. At first, he was afraid they would not understand, then he became afraid that they *would* understand. Also, there was a bright side to be considered; he did enjoy receiving phone calls. He would have preferred to have a live human being on the other end, of course—more specifically, he would have preferred the tinkling voice of Rosalie Mondle on the other end—but there was something reassuring about the jangling of the telephone, no matter who was calling. (And the people next door seemed to look at him with new respect when he passed them in the hall on the way to the incinerator.) Once, a lady with a pleasant voice called to say that T.W.A. reservations would be with him in a moment, and, after quite a few moments, T.W.A. reservations were still not with him. But he didn't get angry; he didn't really want to talk to T.W.A. reservations anyway. Most of the other callers had helpful and interesting information. Although it was unusual, even somewhat disturbing, to be receiving calls constantly from recorded voices, there was the advantage of having a private weather service to be considered. Also, he had more to dream about in the long night spells between Rosalie dreams. He developed a new series of recurring dreams, in which his recorded callers talked to each other on the phone, while he listened contentedly, like a wise host who has just brought together two people who established an instant rapport. "Good morning," a pleasant but confident male voice said at the beginning of one dream. "This is a report from New York's Municipal Communications Service."

"At the tone, the standard time will be eleven-fourteen and forty seconds," ME 7-1212 replied, trying to hide her excitement behind a businesslike voice.

"Traffic is generally moderate," New York's Municipal Communications Service went on, sensing her interest. "The Gun Hill Road exit of the Mosholu Parkway is closed."

"At the tone, the standard time will be eleven-fourteen and fifty seconds," ME 7-1212 said cheerfully, too happy in her new relationship to worry about the Mosholu Parkway.

"Alternate-side-of-the-street parking regulations are in effect today and will be in effect tomorrow."

"At the tone, the standard time will be eleven-fifteen, exactly," ME 7-1212 said. She suddenly sounded a bit stuffy. Was she unable to afford a garage? Barnett wondered. Revelations of character had always interested him.

Then, one day, while Barnett was awake, a voice called with the wrong weather. She told Barnett that it was clear and very warm, with the high in the mid to upper nineties. When he walked out of his apartment in the cord suit he had been saving for the first really hot weather, he discovered that it was about sixty, with a chill drizzle blowing in from the river. He found the experience unsettling.

"You're just going too far, phoning weather information in Albuquerque," Greta Mohler said to her husband that night as he was about to fall asleep.

"I phoned Albuquerque on Sunday," Bernie said. "It's a maximum of a dollar all day on three-minute station-to-stations from anywhere in the country."

"At least they were giving him the right information before," Greta said. "Now, along with not saying beep to him, you're lying to him. It's not funny."

"How come you thought it was funny when the voice called and told him the number he had reached was not a working number?" Bernie asked.

"I heard you recording Dial-A-Prayer today, Bernie," Greta said, ignoring the question. "I don't think you should play that to Barnett."

"Do you really think it's that much worse than your idea of playing him a voice from the Save A Cat League?" Bernie asked.

"I never suggested that."

"It was a perfectly natural thing to mention after I talked about the recorded bird watchers' report from Boston," Bernie said. "When I phoned you from the office that first day, you just got carried away in the excitement."

"I never uttered that suggestion," Greta said.

Bernie got out of bed, switched on the light, found his tape recorder, and played a tape of Greta suggesting that they play Barnett a voice from the Save A Cat League. "I just happened to be practicing at the time," he explained.

He put away the tape recorder, turned out the light, and got back in bed. Greta did not speak. When Bernie left for work the next morning, she still had not spoken.

She remained silent that evening as Bernie, holding the tape recorder at the ready next to the telephone mouthpiece, dialed Barnett's number. When Barnett answered, Bernie flipped on the tape and smiled in Greta's direction as the florid voice of the Dial-A-Prayer prayer reader relayed the Lord's teachings on sin and forgiveness. Occasionally, Bernie and Greta could hear Barnett's quiet interjections of "Yeah" or "Right" or "Good point." The voice on the tape changed so smoothly that Bernie did not even register the difference until halfway through the first sentence. "And we ask forgiveness of Bernie Mohler, betrayer of friends, who holds this tape recorder in his hand," Greta's voice said calmly as Bernie stared down at the tape recorder in his hand. "At the tone, the time will be eight-fifteen, exactly, and Bernie Mohler will be making a fool of himself. Beep."

A week later, on Saturday, Bernie got a call from Barnett. "I forgive you," Barnett said. "You're a victim of technological advancement. I hope it's O.K. between you and Greta."

"We're on our way to Staten Island for an outing and truce negotiations," Bernie said. "It's too bad you and Municipal Communications Service are no longer pals. I was going to ask you about the Staten Island ferry schedule."

"Staten Island ferries are on time," said Barnett. "I phone

999-1234 quite a bit these days. Also the weather and the time. I was sort of missing them. The precipitation probability is down to fifteen per cent, and the barometer is two-nine-point-six-six and steady, if you're thinking about a picnic."

"Thanks very much," Bernie said. "You saved me two message units right there."

"I've been thinking," Barnett said. "I'm going to phone Rosalie this afternoon. If those complete strangers could call me, I should be able to call the girl I want to call. At least it'll be an experience."

"I think this whole thing has been good for you, Barnett," Bernie said.

After Bernie had hung up, Barnett dialed Rosalie's number, which he had known by heart for several years.

"This is Rosalie Mondle," the voice on the other end of the phone said after the third ring.

"This is Barnett," he replied cautiously. "Barnett Frummer."

"I am on tape," the voice went on. "I am not in the house right now, but I'll be returning shortly. If you wish to leave a message, please speak clearly into the phone after the first tone signals. Thank you."

"It's nothing," Barnett mumbled, answering the tone. "I just thought you might be interested in knowing what's at the R.K.O. 86th Street."